EXPLORER ACADEMY

THE DRAGON'S BLOOD

TRUDI TRUEIT

UNDER THE *Stars*

NATIONAL GEOGRAPHIC

FOR DEBBIE, WITH LOVE —TT

NATIONAL GEOGRAPHIC and Yellow Border Design are trademarks of the National Geographic Society, used under license.

Under the Stars is a trademark of National Geographic Partners, LLC.

Since 1888, the National Geographic Society has funded more than 14,000 research, conservation, education, and storytelling projects around the world. National Geographic Partners distributes a portion of the funds it receives from your purchase to National Geographic Society to support programs including the conservation of animals and their habitats. To learn more, visit natgeo.com/info.

For more information, visit nationalgeographic.com, call 1-877-873-6846, or write to the following address:

National Geographic Partners, LLC
1145 17th Street N.W.
Washington, DC 20036-4688 U.S.A.

For librarians and teachers: nationalgeographic.com/books/librarians-and-educators

More for kids from National Geographic: natgeokids.com

National Geographic Kids magazine inspires children to explore their world with fun yet educational articles on animals, science, nature, and more. Using fresh storytelling and amazing photography, *Nat Geo Kids* shows kids ages 6 to 14 the fascinating truth about the world—and why they should care. **kids.nationalgeographic.com/subscribe**

For rights or permissions inquiries, please contact National Geographic Books Subsidiary Rights: bookrights@natgeo.com

Designed by Eva Absher-Schantz
Codes and puzzles developed by Dr. Gareth Moore

Hardcover ISBN: 978-1-4263-7166-0
Reinforced library binding ISBN: 978-1-4263-7167-7

Printed in Hong Kong
21/PPHK/1

PRAISE FOR THE EXPLORER ACADEMY SERIES

"A fun, exciting, and action-packed ride that kids will love."

—J.J. Abrams, award-winning film and
television creator, writer, producer, and director

"Inspires the next generation of curious kids to go out into our world and discover something unexpected."

—James Cameron, National Geographic
Explorer-in-Residence and acclaimed filmmaker

"…a fully packed high-tech adventure that offers both cool, educational facts about the planet and a diverse cast of fun characters."

—Kirkus Reviews

"Thrill-seeking readers are going to love Cruz and his friends and want to follow them on every step of their high-tech, action-packed adventure."

—Lauren Tarshis, author of the I Survived series

"Absolutely brilliant! Explorer Academy is a fabulous feast for mind and heart—a thrilling, inspiring journey with compelling characters, wondrous places, and the highest possible stakes. Just as there's only one planet Earth, there's only one series like this. Don't wait another instant to enjoy this phenomenal adventure!"

—T.A. Barron, author of the Merlin Saga

"Nonstop action and a mix of full-color photographs and drawings throughout make this appealing to aspiring explorers and reluctant readers alike, and the cliffhanger ending ensures they'll be coming back for more."

—School Library Journal

"Explorer Academy is sure to awaken readers' inner adventurer and curiosity about the world around them. But you don't have to take my word for it—check out Cruz, Emmett, Sailor, and Lani's adventures for yourself!"

—LeVar Burton, actor, director, author, and host
of the PBS children's series Reading Rainbow

"Sure to appeal to kids who love code cracking and mysteries with cutting-edge technology."

—Booklist

"I promise: Once you enter Explorer Academy, you'll never want to leave."

—Valerie Tripp, co-creator and author
of the American Girl series

"…the book's real strength rests in its adventure, as its heroes…tackle puzzles and simulated missions as part of the educational process. Maps, letters, and puzzles bring the exploration to life, and back matter explores the 'Truth Behind the Fiction'…This exciting series…introduces young readers to the joys of science and nature."

—Publishers Weekly

"Both my 8-year-old girl and 12-year-old boy LOVED this book. It's fun and adventure and mystery all rolled into one."

—Mom blogger, Beckham Project

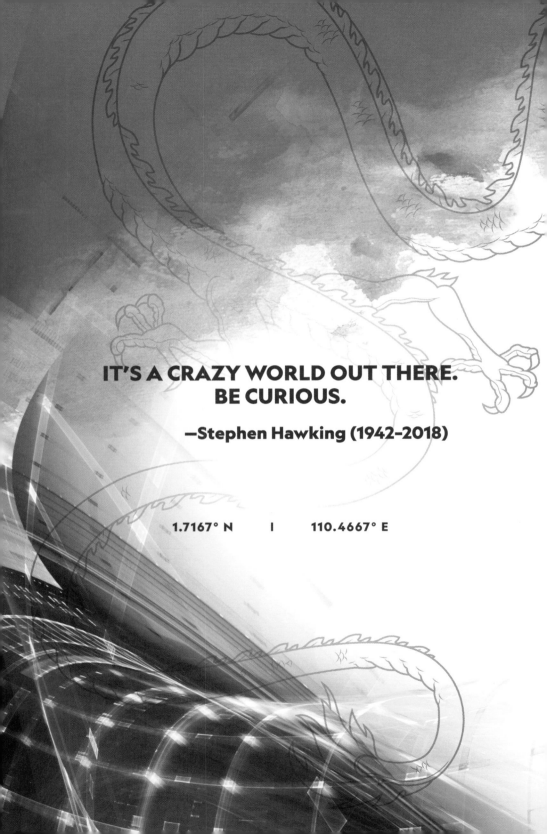

**IT'S A CRAZY WORLD OUT THERE.
BE CURIOUS.**

—Stephen Hawking (1942–2018)

1.7167° N   I   110.4667° E

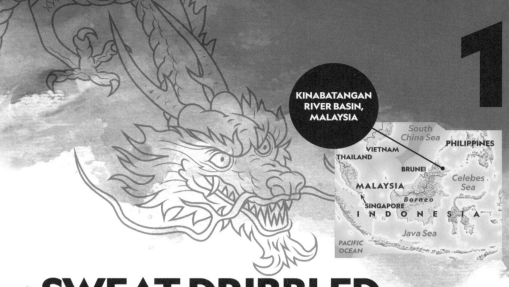

KINABATANGAN
RIVER BASIN,
MALAYSIA

South
China Sea   PHILIPPINES
VIETNAM
THAILAND
                BRUNEI   Celebes
MALAYSIA   Sea
                    Borneo
SINGAPORE
I N D O N E S I A
                Java Sea
PACIFIC
OCEAN

▶**SWEAT DRIBBLED** down the back
of a sticky neck. Hot feet swelled inside boots that got tighter with
each step. Even breathing was hard, like trying to inhale with a wet
towel covering your face. If this was immortality, thought Cruz, it was
way overrated.

Cruz Coronado may have been trekking through a steamy rainforest
in northern Borneo with the explorers and faculty of Explorer Academy,
but his mind was thousands of miles away.

More than two weeks had passed since he'd been inside the Society's
top secret Archive for a glimpse of his mother's scientific logbook.
A single page, the one his PANDA unit had partially revealed, was all the
Synthesis had allowed him to see. Even so, it was enough for Cruz to
finally read his mom's full entry. In it, she explained that she'd handled
her cell-regeneration serum without gloves. A scratch on her hand had
exposed her unborn child—Cruz—to the liquid. The mishap had likely
altered his developing DNA. In short, it was possible he would live . . .

Forever.

It was a stunning discovery. And yet, somehow, it wasn't. Looking
back, Cruz realized he'd hardly been sick a day in his life. Bumps,
bruises, sprains, and other minor injuries had always been quick to
heal. Cruz had figured he'd simply been lucky, but now he knew it was
more than that. So much more.

In her notes, his mother had predicted the full power of the serum would kick in when Cruz turned 13. Apparently, it had—and just in time for him to do battle with Nebula, too. The gash Cruz had gotten on his leg when Prescott nearly drowned him in Hawaii, the burn on his arm from Mr. Rook's laser blast, and his broken toe and concussion from the fall into the cavern in Turkey had all mended within a day or two—faster than ever. Not that Cruz had given any of these injuries much thought when they'd occurred. Now they were all he could think about.

Damaged cells need time to regenerate, right? Cruz figured he was as human as anyone else when it came to things that would cause a quick death, which Nebula must have known, too. Is that why his mother had not survived the fire in her lab? Her cells couldn't repair her injuries fast enough? Or, as an adult, had the serum affected her differently? Cruz had millions of questions, but how was he supposed to get any of them answered when the Synthesis wouldn't let him see the rest of the logbook? Emmett was the only one who knew Cruz had been inside the Archive, though he had no idea what Cruz had learned there—and he could never know. No one could, not even Dad or Aunt Marisol.

"Ow!" yelped Lani.

Cruz had bumped her calf. "Sorry."

Lani was stopped on the trail, her head tipped back. Cruz followed her gaze, his eyes roving up the tangle of thick branches that wove the canopy in layers too numerous to count. Here and there the leaves parted, allowing thin beams of sunlight to slip through. Fruits and flowers punctuated the greenery like red, yellow, and white exclamation points. Squinting, Cruz searched the limbs. "Lani, what are you—"

There! Among the leaves still glossy from an overnight rain, Cruz spotted a patch of reddish gray. A monkey! Its back to them, the animal was crouched on the fork of a twisted tree trunk about 20 feet up. The bright orange-red fur on its head, neck, and shoulders turned a soft gray as it extended down its arms, legs, and tail. The monkey's thin tail was nearly as long as its body. A gray hand with long fingers lazily plucked unripened figs from a tree. By now, Professor Ishikawa had seen the animal, too. He was pointing up, trying to quietly alert everyone to what was above.

Crack!

Someone behind Cruz stepped on a twig. Turning its shoulders, the monkey glanced down and the explorers began to chuckle. The monkey had the biggest nose Cruz had ever seen! Long and droopy, the appendage hung past its mouth like a giant orange pendulum.

"That's a proboscis monkey," whispered their teacher, hushing them. "That nose might seem funny to you, but I can assure you that lady monkeys find it quite attractive."

That got even more giggles.

"Proboscis monkeys are excellent swimmers," added Professor Luben. "His fingers and toes are partially webbed. They help him out-swim crocodiles, one of his main predators."

Once the monkey had finished eating, he reached for a shaggy vine. Pushing himself off the V-shaped trunk, he swung his bulging potbelly toward another branch, stretched a thin, hairy arm out to catch it ...

And missed!

This time, Professor Ishikawa didn't attempt to quiet their laughter. "They're not always as graceful on land," he said.

Cruz spotted another smaller monkey on the second tree. It had a much shorter nose. "There's a female," whispered Professor Luben.

When momentum brought the vine back, the female caught the male by his leg and pulled him onto her limb. The pair began to climb and were soon lost in the dense foliage of the canopy.

As the group continued on, Cruz glanced back, looking for Aunt Marisol's tan-and-pink safari hat. He was close to the front, while she'd brought up the rear. There she was—yep, still near the back. All their teachers had joined them for their hike through Borneo's Kinabatangan River Basin. Cruz suspected it meant they would be breaking up into teams for a mission. His hunch soon proved correct. Another half mile up the trail, Monsieur Legrand, who was leading them, stopped next to a grassy bog. "We'll take a short water and snack break here, then hand out your assignments," he announced.

Cruz rested his backpack against a cracked log, which was being used as a freeway by a line of busy termites. He pulled off one glove to pop open his water bottle, lifted the aluminum canister to his lips, and let the icy water flow down his raw throat. The chill that hit his stomach sent a welcome shiver through him. Ahhhh! Catching a whiff of lavender, Cruz watched Sailor take the top off the bottle of Fanchon's organic mosquito repellent. "You're really layering that stuff on," he said, taking another swig.

"You can't be too careful." Sailor lifted her chin, closed her eyes, and spritzed.

"What is that—four layers now?" teased Cruz.

"Five." When he laughed, she said, "Don't come crying to me when you're covered in welts."

"You do know it has catnip in it, don't you?" said Emmett.

Sailor's eyelids flew open. "It does?"

"It's one of the active ingredients."

"Great," grunted Dugan. "You'll repel the mosquitoes but attract the leopards."

Cruz laughed, nearly spitting water all over Bryndis. She dodged out of the way in the nick of time but was laughing, too.

Professor Ishikawa was signaling for them to gather round. "You're standing deep in the heart of one of the oldest rainforests on Earth," he explained. "The jungles of Borneo are home to more than two hundred species of mammals and four hundred different kinds of birds that we know of. It's one of the few places in the world where elephants, rhinos, and orangutans all live together." He scanned the semicircle of students. "But your task is not to seek the obvious. Today, your mission will be to look for the rarely seen, even the unknown. On our hike, you've probably trekked past hundreds of creatures without realizing it: spiders, ants, snails, frogs, and so on. They may have been under the leaf litter, tucked into a knothole, or perhaps"—he nodded to a light-pink-and-white orchid next to him—"in plain sight." Professor Ishikawa bent to lightly touch the flower and several petals shrank from his fingertips!

There was a collective gasp as the flower began to move.

"Say hello to the orchid *mantis*," said their teacher. "This insect camouflages itself as part of the blossom in order to catch a meal. He's pretty good at fooling bees, flies, and—by your expressions—explorers. Come take a look."

Upon closer inspection, Cruz was able to make out the bug's long, triangle-shaped head, whisker-thin antennae, and six petal-like legs. But it wasn't easy. The soft blend of pale pink and white on its body so perfectly matched the flower that it was hard to tell where the orchid ended and the mantis began.

"Wow!" Emmett's magnifying emoto-glasses were yellow spirals of amazement. "Professor Ishikawa, how did you ever see him?"

Their professor gave a knowing grin. "Practice. Which is precisely the point of today's mission. Here's how it will work: Each team will be assigned a small section of the rainforest to explore. Use your mind-control cameras to take photos of the animal and plant life you observe in your area. Your cameras are linked to the Academy's library database and will help you identify what you find. Unless, of course, you uncover a new species." His grin widened. "Wouldn't that be something? Be sure to take good field notes on your tablet as well, for your team field

report. Those are due at the beginning of class on Monday. Professors Modi, Coronado, Luben, and Benedict will lead the teams. Monsieur Legrand and I will circulate to check on your progress. Each faculty leader has already been assigned a search area. All that's left to do is match the faculty to teams. Monsieur Legrand?"

All eyes went to their survival instructor, who was lifting a small black velvet bag from his pack. The explorers knew it well. They were going to draw for assignments.

"Remember your survival training," said Monsieur Legrand. He was shaking the fabric pouch to mix the chips inside. "Stay alert. Step carefully. Don't wander away from your team. Keep hydrated. Have I forgotten anything?"

"Bug repellent," called Sailor. When their teacher said, "*Oui. Merci, Sailor,*" she gave her teammates a look of satisfaction.

Monsieur Legrand was holding the bag out to Professor Benedict.

"The team that gets Professor Benedict will have the best photos," Emmett said to Cruz. "She'll have good tips for macrophotography."

Emmett was right, but Cruz was hoping they'd get Aunt Marisol.

The journalism teacher plunged her hand into the sack and brought up a chip. "Team Earhart!" she said.

Professor Modi was next. Cruz held his breath waiting for the verdict. "Galileo."

That left Aunt Marisol and Professor Luben, who was rubbing his gloves. He dipped a hand into the pouch. "I'm with …"

Cruz's pulse quickened. *Come on, Aunt Marisol.*

Lifting his arm, Professor Luben glanced up at the chip in his palm. "Team Cousteau!"

So close!

"Dr. Coronado, that means you're with Team Magellan," said Professor Ishikawa.

As Aunt Marisol passed Cruz, she flipped up the brim of her hat and gave her nephew a smirk that said, *One of these days.*

Cruz gave her an I-sure-hope-so grin in return.

"Explorers, compared to your other missions, I know this may seem easy," said Professor Ishikawa. "But don't take it for granted. A good explorer needs sharp observation skills. It takes patience to learn to look beyond the tip of your nose, but when you do"—he motioned to the orchid mantis—"it can make all the difference."

"Did he say tip of your *nose*?" Lani nudged Cruz. "We should name this mission Operation Proboscis."

"Splendid idea, Lani!" Professor Ishikawa swung around. "That's what we'll call it: Operation Proboscis."

Lani smiled so hard her eyes disappeared.

"Leaders, you may depart when your team is ready," instructed Professor Ishikawa. "We'll meet at the lodge at four this afternoon."

"Team Cousteau?" Professor Luben motioned for them to gather round. "I have our search coordinates. Dugan, don't forget your hat. Cruz, be sure to put your other glove back on. That goes for the rest of you. Keep as much of yourself covered as possible. We don't need anyone coming down with dengue fever or malaria."

Cruz tucked his water bottle into the side pocket of his pack, pulled up his socks, and slipped on his other glove. Some of the teams were backtracking, but Professor Luben was leading Team Cousteau farther along the trail. Slinging his pack onto his shoulders, Cruz fell into line behind Emmett, who was following Sailor, Bryndis, and Dugan. Lani brought up the rear. After hiking for about 10 minutes, they took a fork. The path quickly narrowed. Thick broadleaf bushes hugged the trail so tightly that they had to turn sideways in some spots to make their way through. As he wriggled past a plant with long purple nettles, Cruz was glad Professor Luben had been so insistent about protecting their skin.

"I've been thinking," Lani whispered into Cruz's ear, "about the clue."

Cruz had been thinking about it, too. Constantly. Not quite two weeks ago, they had unlocked Cruz's mom's journal for the latest hint. "To find the seventh cipher, you must seek both the ordinary and the extraordinary in an object we both hold close to our hearts," a holographic Petra Coronado had directed. "Something others use to forget the past will reveal *your* future. Your destiny is yours to write, Cruzer."

The cipher!

Cruz, Emmett, Lani, and Sailor had agreed the solution had to be the cipher. It was the most extraordinary thing Cruz had that his mom also held dear. But what was ordinary about it? They carefully studied the engraved black marble cipher from every angle, snapping apart the wedges to inspect them individually. However, they didn't find anything that would lead them to the seventh piece. Sailor suggested that Cruz's mom might be referring to his silver holographic dome. After all, it *had* contained the first fragment of the cipher. Cruz had examined it as well but found nothing. He had drawn the line at taking apart the holo-dome. Although Emmett had assured him he could put it back together, Cruz was not willing to take the chance.

Cruz worried that his mother could be talking about something she'd given him a long time ago. Most of his stuff was back home in Kauai. Cruz had his father search his bedroom for books, toys, games, robotics, surfing gear—anything that might fit the description of being both ordinary and extraordinary. Unfortunately, his dad had come up empty. He'd promised to keep looking. Cruz hoped it wasn't something he'd had when he was really young, like a stuffed animal or a picture book. If that was the case, it was likely long gone.

Cruz glanced at Lani as they scooted shoulder to shoulder down the trail. "What is it?"

"She said your destiny was yours to *write*. What if she was referring to one of the pens in her box? Maybe it writes with a special ink or has a clue rolled up inside."

"We thought of that," replied Cruz. "Emmett and I checked the pens. As far as we can tell, they're all basic pens—well, with the ink dried up, of course. One of them was a paintbrush. It has an angled tip, like you'd use for calligraphy. Nothing special about it that we could see."

Lani sighed. "I thought I was onto something. What about you? Any ideas?"

"Nope," said Cruz. "I'm hopeless."

"Not hopeless," she insisted. "Just stuck. You'll get unstuck soon."

"I'd better. If Nebula figures it out before I do—"

"Cruz! Lani!" Professor Luben was waving from a bend in the trail.

They had fallen behind. Hurrying to catch up, they saw the path ended in a thicket. Tall grasses and ferns sprouted out of the ground like giant fountains. Their teacher told them to spread out about 20 feet apart but to keep the person next to them in sight as they explored. Positioned between Sailor and Bryndis, Cruz stepped carefully through the leaf litter. Bending to peer beneath a frond with thick purple stems, he discovered a cluster of about 20 lime green pitcher plants. They reminded him of a school of hungry fish, their oval mouths turned upward and open wide. Unlike the pitcher plants on Mahé in the Seychelles, these had lids that were far too small to cover their openings.

Cruz snapped a few photos. His MC camera identified the plants as *Nepenthes ampullaria,* common name: flask pitcher plant. He learned that this plant collected and digested leaves instead of insects. No wonder their lids were so little. They weren't really necessary! Cruz was going in for a closer shot of the pitcher plants when he spotted a gooey brown string hanging from a leaf. He lifted the leaf with his thumb and saw that the string was actually a worm!

"Hey there, little guy." Cruz went down on one knee. The worm was only about an inch long with yellow and black stripes running lengthwise down its dark brown body. It was using most of its body to reach out to Cruz. Although he wanted to hold it, Cruz remembered his training and resisted. Instead, he took a picture of the friendly worm, then waited for his MC camera to identify it.

Haemadipsa picta, *common name: tiger leech.*

A type of annelid, or segmented worm, the tiger leech feeds on the blood of animals. It has two suckers, one at each end. Attaching its back caudal sucker to the undersides of leaves and underbrush, the leech uses scent, temperature, and vibration to find a host. Often, it will fall onto the neck, shoulders, arms, or hands of hikers, where it withdraws blood using its front oral sucker. A tiger leech bite may be painful and can be difficult to heal.

Cruz drew back. "Sorry, buddy, I'm nobody's dinner."

The leech went out of focus as Cruz read the description in his lens again. *A tiger leech bite may be painful and can be difficult to heal.*

Interesting. Maybe Cruz couldn't tell anyone about his regenerative ability, but nobody said he couldn't do a few experiments on his own, right? He *was* an explorer, after all.

Cruz yanked off his left glove. Was he crazy to do this? Probably. But how else was he supposed to learn what his body was capable of? And what it wasn't?

He spread his fingers and, in slow motion, put out his arm. The worm swayed toward him. Cruz's hand began to tremble. He tried to steady it. The sucking mouth loomed closer, a tiny, eager O. Cruz grimaced as he waited for the leech to strike.

One more inch . . .

2

CRUZ FELT A SHARP sting, but it wasn't the one he expected.

"Crikey!" Sailor had slapped his hand out of the way of the swerving worm. "What are you doing? Don't you know that's a leech?"

"It . . . it . . . is?"

She frowned. "Didn't your MC identify it?"

"Um . . . no. My camera must be . . . uh . . . malfunctioning?"

Swiping his glove up off the ground, Sailor held it out to him. "And you heard Professor Luben. We're supposed to keep our skin covered."

Cruz quickly tugged the glove back on. "I was . . . uh . . . getting some water—"

"Good thing I was here," she chided.

"Can't argue with that," he said to lighten her mood.

Sailor's scowl only deepened. "Cruz, what's with you lately? You've been distracted and weird and"—she flung out an arm toward the leech—"making mistakes you *never* make."

"Can't argue with that either," he muttered to himself.

"Does it have something to do with your trip?"

Still on one knee, Cruz nearly fell over. How did she find out that he'd gone to the Archive? "Uh . . . what do you mean? What trip?"

Sailor let out an exasperated sigh. "When Fanchon led the

16

sightseeing tour to Kuala Lumpur a few weekends ago, you didn't go ashore with us—"

"I explained that," he said defensively. "I wanted to stay on *Orion* and study—"

"Except you didn't. You didn't stay on board."

Unbelievable! Cruz had been so careful to cover his tracks, leaving the ship after all the explorers had gone on the tour, then sneaking back on board two nights later after midnight. Sailor was getting as good as Nebula at this spy stuff.

Determined eyes drilled into his. "What's going on?"

"Nothing." Cruz lifted a shoulder. "Nothing's going on."

"That's real convincing."

Cruz sprang to his feet. "What do you want me to say?"

"You could start with the truth."

"I've told you everything I can."

Sailor's eyebrows shot up. "So, it's something you *can't* tell me?"

Oops. He hadn't meant to say that. Had he? Cruz had to admit he didn't want to keep his immortality a secret for the rest of his life—however long *that* was. But he'd given his word. It was too late to back out now.

"I meant *know*," he corrected. "I've told you everything I *know*. I'm talking about Mom's clue. We're no closer to solving it than we were when we opened the journal almost two weeks ago. *Two weeks, Sailor!* If Jaguar knows about it, that means Nebula has a big head start on me. For all I know, they could have the seventh piece by now." He ran a hand through his hot, damp hair. "So, yeah, I guess I have been kind of distracted and weird and"—he glanced at the leech—"making stupid mistakes."

"I know." The corners of her mouth softened. "And I haven't been much help. Between our midterms and three missions in two weeks and ... well, everything ..."

She meant Taryn. Not only were they missing their friend, but their adviser, too. The things they'd always counted on Taryn to handle, from getting equipment fixed to ordering supplies, were no longer getting done. She'd left a big hole in their lives and hearts and nobody knew how to fill it.

"When we get back, we'll make the clue priority one," vowed Sailor. She lifted her chin. "And for the record, I already know where you went on your secret trip."

He tensed. "You do?"

"Washington, D.C."

Geez, she was *better* than Nebula!

"To see Dr. Fallowfeld," Sailor said proudly.

His mom's colleague at the Synthesis? What would make her think of him? The scientist who had been severely burned in the fire that had killed Cruz's mom had stepped out of the shadows—twice—to warn Cruz about Nebula. However, Dr. Fallowfeld had also revealed that he knew little about the work that Cruz's mom had been doing and could be of no help to him. Cruz hadn't thought about Dr. Fallowfeld in some time.

"Besides the Synthesis, he's the only one who might know more about the logbook entry," concluded Sailor. "Oh, I know he *said* he wasn't collaborating with your mom, but he was obviously lying."

He was?

"How do you— I mean, how did you figure that out?" asked Cruz.

"If Dr. Fallowfeld *really* didn't know anything, then there would be no reason for him to pretend he died in the lab fire," she reasoned. "Remember, your mom told us she wasn't sure you could trust the Synthesis, which means there had to be someone there who was feeding Nebula critical information. And if there's one thing we know about Nebula, it's that they're not going to waste time chasing somebody with no knowledge of the formula."

She had a point.

"Sooooo?" pressed Sailor. "What did he say?"

Cruz couldn't tell her why he'd really traveled to D.C. If she chose to think he'd gone to see Dr. Fallowfeld, he didn't see any harm in letting her continue to believe it. It was better than an outright lie.

Cruz looked down at the scuffed toes of his hiking boots. "He never showed up."

"Figures. I know you want to find him, but watch out, okay? He could be the one your mom didn't trust. He could be with Nebula."

"I'll be careful," promised Cruz.

Sailor was right. Dr. Fallowfeld had to know more than he'd let on. "Petra would be alive today if she had listened to me," the scientist had said when he'd first confronted Cruz at the Academy. "Nebula can't take the risk that you—" He'd been interrupted before he could finish. What had Dr. Fallowfeld told Cruz's mom? And what couldn't Nebula risk? That Cruz would reach his 13th birthday? That he would find the cipher? Both? Something else?

Cruz knew he needed to find Dr. Fallowfeld. But how? He had no idea where to even begin looking. But maybe there *was* someone who could help . . .

Cruz saw a flash of brown. Sailor had seen it, too. Bluish brown wings were sailing toward them. However, instead of blocking the sun, its feathers filtered it. Transparent wings? Strange. Cruz counted four frog-like legs, one pair extended in front of the wings, the other behind them. Even stranger! When he spotted a long, slender tail, everything made sense. "That's not a bird," called Cruz. "It's a flying lizard!"

As the reptile skimmed their heads, the pair began taking photos. Like a miniature parachute jumper, the lizard glided in for a graceful landing on a nearby tree branch. It easily folded its skin flaps into the sides of its mottled brown body to become a normal lizard once again. It was less than a foot long but seemed much bigger in the air with its flaps spread out, thought Cruz. The two explorers crept toward the tree.

"My MC camera says it's a *Draco volans*. A common flying dragon," whispered Sailor. "The yellow dewlap under its chin and the blue on its skin flaps indicate that it's male."

Cruz was getting the same information on his camera feed. "I didn't know they could glide up to thirty feet—"

"So, it's working now?"

"Huh?"

"Your MC camera? You can see the ID data?"

"Oh...yeah. Yeah. Must have been...uh...a glitch. It's fine now."

"Good," said Sailor, but she was scowling again.

"JOYAH, HOW DO YOU SAY 'DELICIOUS'** in Malay?" Aunt Marisol called to the woman in a white blouse with short puffy sleeves and a red flowing skirt scurrying past.

"Lazat," answered their server, easily balancing a large tray filled with glasses above her head.

A chorus of *"Lazat!"* went up from all five tables.

Seated across from Emmett, Zane, and Ali, and between Lani and Bryndis, Cruz added his voice to the cheer. The hinava was tasty! Cruz took another bite of the cold salad with sliced mackerel, chilies, diced red onions, and bitter gourds. Joyah had explained that the traditional Malaysian dish was seasoned with lime, ginger, and seeds from bamban-gan, a bright yellow mango found only in Borneo.

Having met at Muhibbah Lodge following their mission, the explorers and faculty were eating dinner outside on the inn's huge deck. Built on pilings, the weathered gray deck spanned a good 30 yards along the banks of the muddy Kinabatangan River. Frothy palms, pink orchids, and red rhododendrons burst from pots that lined the railings. Guests could relax on one of the many benches, chaises, or wicker chairs, or, like the explorers, take shelter from the still blistering evening sun by dining at the tables under the red A-frame roof.

Cruz had barely finished the hinava when his salad plate was quietly and quickly replaced by a dinner plate containing a banana leaf folded into a large green triangle.

"This is called nasi lemak," said Joyah, setting a similar pyramid in front of Bryndis.

Cruz wondered what he was supposed to do. Pick it up? Cut into it?

Joyah bent, her long dark hair brushing Cruz's shoulder. "Open it," she said gently.

Cruz began unfolding his banana leaf the way you'd unwrap a gift you hadn't expected. As the leaf unfurled, it released a scent of coconut and roses. Inside, a mound of white rice was surrounded by clusters of different toppings: toasted peanuts, sliced cucumbers, fried anchovies, half a hard-boiled egg, and a spoonful of chunky red sauce.

"That's sambal." Joyah gave Cruz a devilish grin when she saw him dip his fork into the sauce. "Careful. It's a bit on the spicy side."

"I like spicy," said Cruz.

"I *love* spicy," snapped Ali, narrowing his eyes at Cruz.

Was that a dare?

Challenge accepted.

Exchanging his fork for a spoon, Cruz scooped up as much sambal as would fill the utensil. Cruz gave Ali a look of defiance before putting the whole thing in his mouth. A half second later, his entire head felt like it was on fire!

As if she'd seen this scene before, Joyah turned and picked up a glass pitcher of milk and a set of tall glasses, lying in wait off to the side. "Drink this. It will help," she urged, trying to stifle her laughter.

Cruz flung out a hand for his milk. It took most of the liquid in the glass to put out the flames that engulfed him. His throat, his tongue, and even his lips were burning. Meanwhile, a forkful of rice and a smidge of sambal hovered in front of Ali's mouth. Through watery eyes, Cruz watched Ali slowly lower his hand. Ali turned his wrist, and the rice and sambal dropped onto his plate. Cruz sat back, his sizzling lips managing to form a faint grin. Victory was his.

For dessert, there were trays of kuih-muih, small cakes, cookies, and pastries. Cruz tried a pineapple tart and some batang buruk, unfilled spring rolls fried to a light crisp and dusted with sugar and mung bean powder. Both were *lazat*! Emmett reached for pinjaram, a little saucer-shaped fried cake made of rice flour, wheat flour, sugar, and green food coloring. He held it up. "It looks like a spaceship!"

Joyah laughed. "We do call them UFO cakes."

Emmett bit into his fritter. "It's out of this world."

That got a chorus of groans from the table.

After dinner, Monsieur Legrand instructed everyone to collect their gear and make their way to the boat ramp. Several of the lodge's tour boats were waiting to take them downriver to where *Orion* was anchored in the Sulu Sea. As the others got up, Cruz hung back. He motioned for Emmett to do the same. Once they were alone in the shelter, Cruz told Emmett about his conversation with Sailor. "She knew I went to Washington, D.C."

"What?"

"She doesn't know about the Archive. She thinks I went to see Dr. Fallowfeld."

Joyah and a couple of the bus staff were coming to clear away their dishes. Grabbing their packs, Cruz and Emmett strolled across the giant deck toward the steps that led to the dock.

"I told Sailor that we never met up . . . that I couldn't find him," continued Cruz. "But now I do. Need to find him, I mean. I'm pretty certain he knows more about my mom's work than he admitted."

Emmett eyed him. "I get it. And you want my mom's help."

"She *is* the director of the Synthesis."

"Shhhh!" Emmett glanced around the post they were passing. "Even if she could locate him, I doubt she'd tell you where he is. It's most likely classified info."

"Okay, what if we let *him* track *me* down?" asked Cruz. "Your mom could send him a message saying that I have to talk to him, couldn't she? Couldn't she do that?"

Emmett pursed his lips. "Maybe."

Cruz stifled a scream. Maybe wasn't good enough. How could he make his friend understand how important this was without revealing what he'd learned at the Archive? "I wish I could explain, Emmett. All I can say is that it's a matter of life and—" Cruz let out a nervous chortle. He had been about to say "death."

Emmett's emoto-glasses were turning into sapphire trapezoids. Puffs of pink and aqua burst inside the frames like dandelion seeds in the wind. "I'll do my best."

He was sincere. Curious, a little concerned, and slightly nervous, but truthful.

"Thanks." Cruz wanted to say more but knew he couldn't. And Emmett knew it, too.

They'd reached the end of the wood deck. Trotting down the steps, they joined everyone on the pier. Above them, the first stars of the evening winked in the violet sky. Lani was fishing around in her backpack. When she came up, Cruz saw she'd put on her night-vision goggles. "Smart," he said. Lani was always prepared. Their instructions had said this was to be a daytime mission, so Cruz had not thought to bring his own glasses.

"I thought we might see a clouded leopard." Lani adjusted the frames on her nose. "I know it's crazy. They're solitary and elusive and it's a one-in-a-billion chance that I'd ever spot one, but still . . ."

"You gotta try," finished Cruz.

The glasses bobbed up and down.

Once the other explorers saw Lani, those who'd brought night-vision gear began digging it out, too. Cruz watched Felipe unfold a pair of EA standard-issue frames. After using his high-tech night-vision goggles in an attempt to steal the cipher, was Felipe now trying to pretend he didn't have them? Or maybe he knew Cruz had set a trap for him in *Orion*'s laundry room and had gotten rid of the evidence.

Sailor had noticed, too. She nudged Cruz as if to say, *Watch this.* "Hey, Felipe, where's your OptiTek 5000s?"

"At the bottom of the Indian Ocean," he answered.

"It's my fault," interjected Kwento. "I was telling Felipe all about our EggsTend invention, and I accidentally knocked them off our rail."

"Awww, that's too bad," said Sailor. "You just got those."

"Tell me about it." Felipe sighed.

"I said I'd replace them," said Kwento.

"And I said you didn't have to," said Felipe. "You didn't mean to do it."

Cruz frowned at Kwento. "Did you say it happened when you were telling Felipe about EggsTend?"

"Yep, that Funday afternoon right after we finished our robotics activity with Taryn."

Cruz nodded. If Felipe's spy glasses had taken a dive right after midwinter break, then he couldn't have been wearing them two weeks later when Cruz and his friends had set up their trap to catch Nebula's agent in the laundry room.

Cruz locked eyes with Emmett, whose emoto-glasses were flashing red, gold, and green faster than a broken traffic signal. They were both thinking the same thing. Cruz had suspected for a while that Felipe might not be the explorer spy, and now he had confirmation. Jaguar was still out there. Or, more accurately, right here. On this very dock.

A chill creeping down his spine, Cruz let his eyes wander over the crowded pier. He didn't see another pair of OptiTek 5000s. Not that he expected to. The spy was far too clever to use them here. Cruz watched the explorers talking and laughing as they began to board the canoe-like boats. His eyes traveled over the group: Zane, Kwento, Ali, Matteo, Dugan, Tao, Shristine, Kat...

Who was it?

Which one of them was betraying him to Nebula?

3

►**"SERIOUSLY?"** Hezekiah Brume let out a double snort. "You couldn't find a kid in a library?"

In Prescott's defense, it was the world's largest library. He wasn't, however, foolish enough to say this to his boss. Instead, he set his jaw and stared at the sapphire slab that filled the screen of his phone. To keep his identity hidden, the head of Nebula Pharmaceuticals had turned his camera lens toward a blue granite counter. Silver and white flecks swirled within the stone like a miniature Milky Way.

"Cobra, what in the blazes happened?" demanded Brume.

Prescott had no idea. Things had started out routinely enough. Zebra had alerted him that Cruz was on his way to Washington, D.C., to find his mother's scientific logbook. It was located in some library, said their agent on board Orion. Prescott had hightailed it to the nation's capital, catching up to Cruz at the airport as he was being met outside the terminal by Emmett's father. Prescott had followed them as they drove to the Jefferson Building at the Library of Congress. Of course! That was the archive Zebra had meant.

Prescott watched them enter the library. Rather than go in, too, and be spotted, he parked across the street from Dr. Lu's vehicle and waited. That's where things started to go south. The pair never came out. Three hours into his surveillance, another man walked up to Dr. Lu's car, got in, and drove off. Prescott stayed on his tail. After a 45-minute drive that took him in circles, he ended up back at the airport. The man dropped off the vehicle at a rental agency, then vanished into the crowded airport.

Prescott told his boss the only thing that made sense. "They must have seen me."

Brume grumbled something he couldn't hear. "And the logbook? Does Cruz have it?"

"I . . . um . . . don't know. He might." Prescott heard something smash against a hard surface. A fist against stone? The crash knocked the phone askew on its stand. He could now see a corner of the wall mirror and, in it, the reflection of a tanned hand clenched atop a dark blue countertop with comet-like swirls. "Do you want me to—"

"I'll take care of it," growled Brume. "You're to stay on task. Go for the cipher. Stand by for instructions from Zebra. I'll be sending reinforcements."

Reinforcements? He knew what that meant. Prescott was going to get stuck with Komodo and Scorpion again. Not exactly Hawking and Einstein. Those two had bungled the kidnapping and pretty much everything else Brume had given them to do. But they worked cheap and kept their mouths shut—two factors that appealed to his boss.

Zebra, too, was starting to trouble him, but for very different reasons. Their mole on board Orion was intelligent, ambitious, and coy. Lately, she had been communicating with him less and less. He had the feeling a power struggle was going on, and he was on the losing end. "It would help if I could touch base directly with Jaguar rather than going through Zebra," said Prescott. "It would avoid confusion and—"

"No. We can't afford to scare this one."

That was a strange way to put it. Could it be that their explorer spy was having doubts? Or had been pressured into being an agent for Nebula? It had never occurred to Prescott that Jaguar might not be a willing participant.

"Zebra will look after Jaguar," said Brume. "You'll handle the end game."

Naturally. It wasn't enough to get rid of Cruz. Jaguar would have to be dealt with, too. Their explorer spy was a part of this whole ugly tapestry, and Brume couldn't afford to leave any loose threads.

The image on Prescott's screen was shaking. Brume was readjusting his phone. The mirror disappeared, and Prescott was facing the granite counter again. This time, he saw something different in the stone: a faint trail of silver streaking through the galaxy, a lone comet disappearing into the deep blue.

4

"CRUZ!"

Halfway up the atrium's grand staircase, he turned. Aunt Marisol was crossing the inlaid-wood compass design in the center of the floor, her dark ponytail swinging purposefully from side to side. In black jeans, a black long-sleeved shirt with a high white collar and white cuffs, his aunt reminded him of a tuxedo cat. Circular, hammered steel earrings caught the midday sun streaming in through the skylight, reflecting splashes of light onto the curved maple wood walls. A pair of bright yellow sandals with a row of white silk daisies bridging the toes clicked up the stairs. "Did you hear?" she asked. "Looks like Team Magellan might have found a new species on the mission."

A pang of envy stabbed him in the gut. "Oh yeah? That's terrific." Cruz tried to sound enthusiastic, but it came out thin and whiny, like the air slowly being let out of a balloon.

"Ali discovered a moth," said his aunt. "If it's confirmed, he'll get to name it, naturally."

"I'll tell Team Cousteau." He wagged his tablet. "I'm on my way to the library." It was Sunday afternoon. Their field report was due tomorrow.

"Me too." She put an arm around his shoulders, and they continued up the steps. "Don't look so depressed. It's not a competition."

He gave her a sideways look that said, *It is so and you know it.*

Aunt Marisol bent, her heavy earrings smacking her jaw. "Do you have a sec?"

"Uh … sure." Cruz knew what she wanted to discuss, and he'd been dreading it.

At the top of the staircase, she steered him toward an empty corner of the lounge. "Have you solved the clue yet?"

"Um … n-not quite," he stammered, glancing down at the silk daisies on Aunt Marisol's sandals. Each white flower had a small yellow jewel in its center. "We need a little more time."

"A little is all you've got if you want to do it before we leave Sandakan. We're putting to sea tomorrow."

"Tomorrow?" gulped Cruz.

"We can't hold up the sailing schedule any longer."

"Where are we going?"

"It's a surprise," she said mysteriously. "You'll find out with the rest of the explorers in class. But don't worry. I'm sure Dr. Hightower will make sure you get to wherever the clue leads."

Cruz wasn't as certain. The president of the Academy had recently expressed concern over the amount of class time Cruz, Sailor, Emmett, and Lani were missing each time they went in search of a piece of the stone. Cruz knew that the longer he took to complete the cipher, the shorter her patience was likely to be. They needed to solve the seventh clue. And soon.

Aunt Marisol was squinting at him. "Must be a tough one, huh?"

"You have no idea. Mom said to look for something the two of us hold close that's both ordinary and extraordinary. We're pretty sure the extraordinary part is the stone, but we don't know—"

"You've analyzed it, right?"

"Uh-huh. The PANDA unit identified it as black marble from Mexico." Cruz's head shot up so fast, a cramp stung his neck. "You think Mom wants me to go to Mexico?"

She thought about it, then shook her head. "Probably not. Since PANDA units weren't around eight years ago, even she couldn't have accurately pinpointed the stone's country of origin. Did Petra say anything else?"

"She said something people used to forget the past will reveal my future and that my destiny was mine to write."

"That's it?"

"That's it."

A vertical crease appeared between her brows. "Rather cryptic, isn't it?"

"Now you see our problem."

"I sure do."

They heard voices. Dr. Vanderwick and Fanchon came into the lounge. Both waved before taking seats on the opposite side of the compartment. Cruz and his aunt waved back. She turned him toward the stairs. "Come on."

The two made their way up two flights to the bridge deck. Inside the library, Cruz glanced up and saw Bryndis at the second-floor rail.

She smiled. Cruz's stomach flipped. Twice.

"Romeo, there's your Juliet," said his aunt softly as they approached the stairs.

"Aunt Marisol!"

She wore a satisfied smirk, her daisy sandals veering her toward the first-floor bookcases. *"Hasta luego, mi sobrino."*

"Bye, *Tía.*" Cruz took the steps to the balcony two at a time.

He was the last member of Team Cousteau to arrive. His teammates had already settled into their favorite gathering spot. From here, they could see most of the entire first floor: the plump navy chairs nestled in pairs against the portholes, the bookcases built into the mahogany walls with their heavy glass accordion doors, and Dr. Holland's carved mahogany U-shaped desk. Cruz loved being directly below the giant world map that spanned the length of the oval ceiling. Lit by the sun overhead, the glass continents glowed green, purple, and gold. The seas, from the pastel blue along the coasts to the dark cerulean of the deep ocean, swirled and flowed as if pushed by real currents. It was mystical,

almost alive. Cruz never tired of looking at it.

Cruz heard a distant engine but not from beneath his feet, as usual. The map flickered. A shadow. Something was passing between the sun and the ship.

"Helicopter." Lani read his thoughts.

"Cruz, did you hear?" asked Dugan. "Team Magellan found a new species."

Cruz plopped into the open chair between Lani and Sailor next to the brass rail. "I heard."

Dugan slumped down. "I can't believe Ali found a sloth."

"Moth," corrected Bryndis.

"Whatever. All that matters is he found it and we didn't."

"He gets to name it, too," sighed Lani.

Emmett had his head tilted back so far, you could see only his chin. "He'll probably name it Ali's Fantastic Amazing Incredible Moth."

"We'll never hear the end of it," moaned Dugan.

"Come on, guys," rallied Sailor. "You look like a bunch of dried-up jellyfish on the beach. So Ali found a moth. It's not like he discovered an entire *ancient city*." She shot Cruz a look.

"Which I found by accident," mumbled Cruz.

"So did Ali!" she said far too loudly for a library, and quickly lowered her voice. "That's what discoveries are: unexpected finds. And I bet we found some great stuff, too. Everybody bring up your field notes and photos, and let's start on our report. Who wants to go first?"

"I will," said Lani. She held up her screen to show them a photo of a tiny dark brown frog with white spots on its legs and sides. A wide lighter brown stripe, the color of milk chocolate, ran down the center of its back. "I found this guy in the leaf litter. It's a spotted mahogany frog, *Abavorana luctuosa*."

"You should have seen Professor

Luben when she showed it to him." Dugan pushed himself up in his chair. "He said it was rare to see this frog in the wild and went all fireworks on us."

"See?" Sailor knocked on the round table between them. "That's what I'm talking about."

Cruz lightly bumped Lani's knee with his own to say, *Good job.*

She bumped back.

As they went around the circle, Cruz began to feel a little better. They *had* done well. Bryndis had come across a coiled-up pill millipede and a giant walking stick insect that looked so much like a twig, Cruz had a hard time spotting the bug in her photo. Dugan had managed to get some beautiful pictures of a wrinkled hornbill taking cover high in the branches. With perfect focus, he'd zoomed in on the sleek black bird with huge dark eyes and a curving pale yellow neck. An impressive red helmetlike bulge was attached to the top of its golden beak.

Besides the flying dragon and tiger leech, Cruz and Sailor had also seen a colony of *Colobopsis explodens,* aka exploding ants.

"When threatened, the ants protect the nest by rupturing their abdomens," explained Sailor. "The explosion releases a sticky liquid that can kill an attacker."

"Self-destructing ants? Wild!" Dugan held up his hand, and Cruz slapped it. "We did a good job on this mission."

Everyone agreed that Professor Ishikawa wouldn't be disappointed in their report. Even so, the truth was clear: While their discoveries may have been rare, beautiful, or even weird, none was a new species. It looked like, this time, Team Magellan was going to come out on top.

"Hey, check it out." Dugan was waggling his thumb toward the first floor.

Peering between the rails, Cruz saw his aunt sitting in one of the several pairs of chairs that faced each other. Professor Luben was in the chair opposite her. Their teacher appeared to be his usual animated self, gesturing as he talked quietly. Aunt Marisol was leaning forward, listening.

"Betcha they're on a date," said Dugan.

"They are not," said Cruz. "They're probably doing lesson plans."

"I don't see a tablet," sang Dugan. "I still say it's a date. What do you guys think?"

Sailor rested her chin on the lower rail. "They do *kinda* look like—"

"Sailor!" fumed Cruz.

"Sorry, but it wouldn't be the worst thing in the world, would it?"

"Let's finish writing our report," said Bryndis, earning a grateful look from Cruz.

As they worked, Cruz snuck another look at the couple below. They did have a lot in common. Both Aunt Marisol and Professor Luben were archaeologists. Both were teachers. Both enjoyed exploring. Even so, there was a big leap between friendship and love, right? One conversation between two faculty members wasn't enough to convince Cruz that Aunt Marisol had a thing for Professor Luben or vice versa. *But* if she did like him, it would be kind of fun to tease her about Professor Luben the way she always kidded him about Bryndis. Turnabout, as Sailor would say.

"Hey, Cousteau." Zane poked his head around a post. "Did you hear?"

"We know, we know!" Dugan waved him away. "Ali discovered a mosquito—"

"No, well, yes—a moth, actually. But I meant did you hear our new adviser is here! Matteo just messaged me."

"Let's go!" Dugan leaped from his chair.

Lani glanced around the group. "We're done, right?"

"Uh-huh," said Sailor, typing faster. "I'm turning in our field report right now."

Emmett and Bryndis were getting up, too. Cruz wasn't as quick to move as his teammates. He couldn't say why. He'd known this was coming. *Orion*'s explorers needed an adviser, of course. And Taryn would be the first one to say it was time to move on. Cruz could almost hear her. "Word to the wise, explorer, you can't let yesterday take up too much of today." His head told him it made sense. But his heart...

His friends were waiting. Cruz pushed himself out of the chair, tucked his tablet under his arm, and followed them out of the library. Bryndis reached for his hand. His heart skipped. Her fingers were cool in his. On the stairs, they joined the stream of students coming from the tech lab, dining room, and lounges. As usual, news had traveled through the ship at light speed. There wasn't nearly enough room for 24 explorers to squish into the adviser's cabin, so Team Cousteau had to be content to take turns standing on their toes and peering in from the doorway. "I'll come back," Cruz said to Bryndis. "It's time to take Hubbard to his meadow."

She let his hand go, though it didn't seem like she wanted to.

He knew how she felt.

In his cabin, Cruz was greeted by a bouncing Westie with a green ball in his mouth. "Hi, Hub!" Cruz went down on one knee to scratch the dog behind his ears. Hubbard dropped his ball in front of Cruz, who picked it up and gently tossed it toward the veranda door. Hub scurried after it, his paws sliding on the slick floor as he made the tight turn to bring it back. After several more rounds of fetch, Cruz gave Hubbard two dog treats and some fresh water. He clipped the leash on to the pup's collar, and the pair headed to the aft deck next to Cruz and Emmett's cabin for a pit stop. Hubbard needed exercise. Cruz figured he'd stop in to meet the new adviser, then take the dog on a good long walk around the ship.

Arriving at the adviser's cabin, Cruz saw that little had changed in the 15 minutes he'd been gone. The crowd of explorers was still there, and most of Team Cousteau was still stuck in the passageway. Only Sailor had made progress. She'd managed to squeeze between Felipe,

Weatherly, and the rest of Team Galileo to get inside the doorway.

Cruz heard a whimper. Hubbard was tugging on his leash, pulling Cruz toward the cabin. He wanted to go in. This place is—was—his home. He must have thought Taryn was back.

"It's okay, Hub," soothed Cruz.

Hearing the dog's sad pleas, Weatherly, Blessica, Misha, and Felipe moved aside to let Cruz go by. Their sympathetic looks told him they understood. With everyone reaching to pet him, Hubbard calmed down. Cruz scooted in next to Sailor. "Sit, Hubbard," he whispered firmly. "Stay."

Peering between Tao and Femi, Cruz got his first look at their new adviser. She seemed about the same age as Taryn—maybe a year or two older—and a few inches taller. Hair the color of gingersnaps was pulled back into two French braids that trailed down the sides of her head, falling below her collarbone. Her large blue eyes were framed with thick eyelashes so long they nearly touched her eyebrows. In a white sleeveless tank and beige cargo pants, she was working her way toward the door. As their new adviser asked their names and answered questions, a strong honey brown arm reached for the explorers' hands.

"She's twenty-eight, her birthday is September twenty-first, and she's from Prince Rupert, British Columbia," Sailor said to Cruz. "She has Tsimshian roots—that's a Canadian First Nations people. She's an Explorer Academy graduate with college degrees in engineering and oceanography. She helped build submersible robots that could map coral reefs and ice shelves so scientists could measure the impact of climate change and survey endangered species populations."

"Is that it?" joked Cruz when Sailor came up for air.

"No, there's more! She's a vegan, is allergic to peppers, and is not allergic to nuts but doesn't like them. This is her first year as an adviser and she says she's a little nervous about it. She's not married but has a boyfriend named Logan. He's the journalism and photography teacher on board *Endeavor*." Sailor took a big breath. "*That's* all."

Cruz couldn't resist. "Didn't you forget something?"

Sailor munched on her lip. "I don't think so ..."

"What's her name?"

Suddenly, the woman was in front of him. "I'm Nyomie Byron."

"Hi." Cruz took the hand she offered. "Cruz Coronado."

"*Ruff!*"

"And this is Hubbard," Cruz said above the laughter of the other explorers.

"Why, hello there!" She bent. "I've heard a lot about you."

A short white tail wagged at double speed. She ruffled the fur behind his ears, scratching his favorite spot.

"Excuse me, explorers!" A crewman in a black beanie was trying to get through the explorers. He held a pearl-pink hourglass-shaped vase full of sunflowers and sprigs of rosemary.

Cruz flattened himself against the wall so the bouquet could pass. The golden blossoms were as big as his hands. It didn't take long for the sweet scent of rosemary to fill the small room. Flowers this fresh could only come from one place: *Orion*'s greenhouse.

"There's a card," said Bryndis, watching the crewman place the vase on the dresser.

"I bet it's from Dr. Hightower," said Sailor.

"Thank you," said Ms. Byron. She plucked a small pink envelope

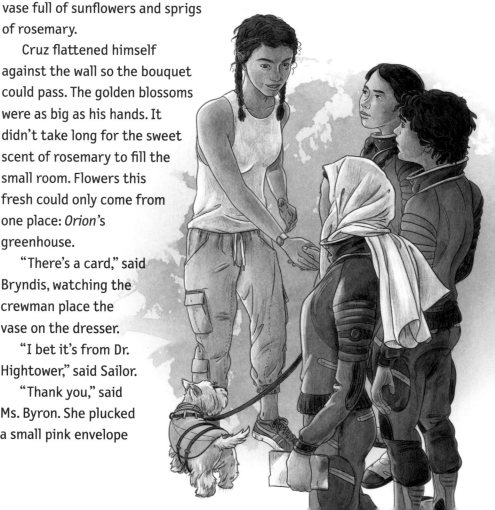

from a pick stuck between the flowers, lifted the flap, and took out the card. Suddenly, the room was quiet. Would she read it out loud? Their new adviser did not disappoint them. "'Welcome to *Orion*! I know the explorers will help you get settled in. Wishing you fair winds and calm seas, R. Hightower.'"

Sailor bounced. "I knew it!"

Their adviser placed the card back into the envelope. "Thanks, explorers, for coming to greet me. I'm looking forward to getting to know each of you better. In the meantime, don't hesitate to let me know how I can assist you."

"Uh … Ms. Byron?" Tao raised her hand. "Did you mean that? 'Cause my comm pin is cutting in and out."

"The battery on my tablet won't hold a charge," said Dugan.

"We have a loose handle in our shower," said Zane.

Several more arms shot up. Their adviser sighed. "You have been on your own for a bit, haven't you? Everyone who needs something, stick around and we'll make a list. However, before you go, there's one thing I absolutely *must* insist upon from every single one of you."

Nobody moved. This sounded serious.

Topaz blue eyes crinkled. "Call me Nyomie, okay?"

Twenty-four explorers let out a sigh of relief. The group began to break up, with those needing help remaining behind. Cruz wanted to mention that his pants were getting a little short, but he didn't want to do it in front of everybody. He'd come back later. Cruz led Hubbard out of the cabin, turning left to go toward the atrium.

"Hey." Ali caught up with him. "Did you hear? I discovered a new species on the mission. A moth. It's bright orange with black eyespots on its wings. I get to name it and everything."

"I heard. That's cool. Congratulations."

Ali puffed out his chest. "You don't believe me?"

"I … I do. I said congratulations, didn't I?"

"Yeah, but it was the *way* you said it."

Cruz wasn't sure how to respond. He *had* meant it. He couldn't help how Ali had heard it, could he? "Uh … what are you going to name it?" asked Cruz half-heartedly. Something past Ali's shoulder had caught his eye—or, rather, some*one*.

It was Emmett. He was still rooted to the same spot in the corridor, still staring into Nyomie's cabin. He had an odd expression on his face.

"I'm not sure yet," said Ali. "Professor Ishikawa says taxonomy is a big deal, so I have to come up with a really good name …"

Emmett's emoto-glasses were changing colors—yellow to blue to green, all with bursts of bubble-gum pink. Something was going on in that brain of his.

"… I'm thinking I'll probably name it after myself," Ali was still chattering. "It looks like it's going to be classified in the *Amata* genus so something like *Amata ali* or maybe *Amata soliman* or I could go with *Amata ali soliman* …"

"Uh-huh … Sounds great." Cruz gently tugged on Hubbard's leash to turn him around. "I … uh … have to go … See you later?"

"I knew you'd be jealous," shot Ali.

Ignoring the remark, Cruz made his way back to Emmett. He waved a hand in front of his friend's blank face. "You seasick?" It was funny, he thought, considering they hadn't left port. Emmett didn't smile. Maybe he *was* sick. When his friend still didn't respond, Cruz's grin faded. "Emmett?"

"I think I've got it," whispered his roommate.

"The flu?"

"The *clue*." Turning to Cruz, Emmett's emoto-glasses became as transparent as the crystals in the atrium chandelier. "But we might be too late."

5

COME ON, *come on!*

Cruz stood half in and half out of cabin 202. His left hand drummed the doorframe, while his right foot tapped the floor. Ten seconds later, Lani scooted past him into the room. Then Sailor. Ducking into the cabin, Cruz shut the door. Everyone turned to Emmett, whose eyes filled his lemon emoto-frames. For once, their shape and color were a match. "Do you guys remember the way we found each piece of the formula?" asked Emmett.

"Sure," answered Lani. "The first stone was in Cruz's holo-dome. I opened that one."

"I'll never forget the second piece," groaned Sailor. "We nearly died in that cave in Iceland—"

"No, no," broke in Emmett. "I didn't mean how *we* found them. I meant how *they* were when we found them."

Confused, Cruz glanced at Lani, who looked at Sailor, who made a face at Cruz. Even Hubbard, resting on Cruz's bed, had his head tilted, though he probably was just hoping for a treat.

Emmett tried again. "When Nyomie took out Dr. Hightower's card, it hit me. When we found the stones, some of them were in envelopes."

Ahhh! Now they understood.

Cruz was the first to add it up. "Three, right? The one at the Byzantine church in Petra—"

"Then behind the photo at the conservation center in Namibia," said Sailor.

"And the one under the Taj Mahal," finished Lani, grinning at Cruz.

"Right," said Emmett. "And it made me wonder, how come only three were in envelopes? Was there something *extraordinary* about them? Then I remembered two of the three were wrapped in paper. Again, I wondered, was there something special about *them*? At first, I thought maybe it was because there wasn't enough room for paper and an envelope in the holo-dome, which made sense, but there *was* plenty of space in the seed packet at Svalbard and in the laughing dragon rock. Then I figured, Cruz, maybe your mom put the paper in to protect the stones, but that seemed unlikely. Marble doesn't need protecting, and if it did, parchment sure wouldn't do the job. The only reason for adding paper to the envelope would be—"

"To send a message!" gasped Lani.

Emmett pointed at her. "Exactly."

"Don't forget, Cruz's mom *did* say his destiny was his *to write*," said Sailor.

All eyes swung to Cruz. Had he kept the pages? Or were they too late?

Cruz calmly crossed to his nightstand. He opened the top drawer and reached to the back corner. Retrieving two of the three aqua envelopes, he handed one to Sailor and the other to Lani.

"You've still got them!" cheered Emmett.

Each of the girls opened her envelope, carefully removing the folded page inside.

Lani flipped hers. "It's blank on both sides."

"Mine, too," said Sailor.

"Sorry to burst your bubble," said Cruz. He'd already inspected them.

"Let me see those." Emmett took both pages, bringing them to within a few inches of his magnification lenses. As he studied them, the emoto-glasses turned to bright orange blobs of frustration. Sailor paced to the porthole. Lani sank onto the edge of the bed. Cruz pretended to straighten his desk.

Sailor whirled. "It could be steganography."

"An invisible message?" shot Cruz.

"Why not? Your mom used glow-in-the-dark paint on your Sossusvlei shirt," she recalled. "She could have done it here, too."

Lani bolted for the porthole. "I'll get the blinds."

"Cabin lights off," ordered Cruz, and the ambient computer obeyed.

Except for the slivers of light slipping through the tops and bottom of the blinds, it was totally dark in the room. All eyes went to the pages in Emmett's hand. Cruz drew in a sharp breath, waiting for words to illuminate his roommate's face. But the only thing glowing was Emmett's yellow frames.

They'd been wrong. There was no secret message.

Disappointed, Cruz finally said, "Lights on."

"Guess that's that." Sailor shuffled to raise the blinds.

"Hold on!" Lani was rapidly twisting the silver stripe in her hair. "Cruz's mom gave the Sossusvlei shirt to Dr. Jo because she knew it would be safe with her. But the stones—well, it's possible those could fall into the wrong hands. I don't know about you guys, but if I wanted to be super careful about how I sent a message, I'd use disappearing ink."

Emmett nodded. "It's easy enough to make your own."

"Anything acidic would work," reminded Sailor. "Milk, vinegar, soda pop, lemon juice, orange juice…"

While she continued rattling off a list of acidic liquids, Cruz scurried to the bathroom to get their hair dryer. He handed it to Lani, then plugged it in. Meanwhile, Emmett and Sailor smoothed down the pages on Emmett's blue granite desk. The explorers knew that the heat from the dryer would create a chemical reaction, freeing the carbon in the acidic "ink" to allow the message—if there was one—to show up on the page in brown print.

Lani pointed the dryer at the desk. "Ready?"

To keep the pages from flying away, Emmett held down one piece of paper while Sailor held the other. "Ready," said Sailor, spreading her fingers.

Lani flipped the switch. The low heat sent gentle ripples through the blue parchment. She directed the heat to the top of the pages, slowly moving over them. Cruz's heart began to thump as he looked for his mom's message to appear. Was that a letter? No. Only a wrinkle. Lani moved the hair dryer down the parchment.

"I don't see anything," said Sailor. "Do you?"

Everyone turned to the person who had the best eyes. Emmett shook his head.

"Flip the pages," suggested Cruz.

They did. Again, nothing.

"I can turn up the heat," suggested Lani.

"Okay, but be careful," warned Emmett. "You don't want to burn the paper."

Lani took a full step back. She clicked the knob up one notch to medium, and the heat began to make waves on the paper. The corners started to curl. Still, the pages remained blank on both sides. After several minutes, Lani glanced up at Cruz. "Keep going?"

The ink should have appeared by now, and they all knew it. Cruz shook his head. Lani shut off the dryer.

"Bummer." Sailor straightened and cracked her back. "I thought for sure we were onto something."

So had Cruz.

Emmett and Sailor gently folded each piece of aqua parchment, now brittle and warped, put them back in their envelopes, and set them on Cruz's nightstand.

They were back to square one, and the clock was ticking. Still, nobody wanted to say those two awful words: What now?

Instead, Emmett said his usual two words. "Anybody hungry?"

"It *is* dinnertime," said Sailor. "How about if we come back and try again after we've had something to eat?"

"Good plan," said Lani, who was winding the cord to the hair dryer.

"You guys go on," said Cruz. "I'll feed Hubbard and catch up."

Alone in his cabin, Cruz took a glass container out of the little fridge next to the closet. Not long after Taryn's death, Fanchon had sent the mini fridge to their cabin. Even though they didn't really have the space for it, Cruz and Emmett had not protested. They knew how important it was to Taryn that Hubbard have fresh, healthy food. Back at the Academy, she'd made most of his meals herself. Once on board *Orion,* Chef Kristos and his staff had taken over preparing the dog's food, but Taryn had been no less involved. She'd supervised every aspect of it, often to Chef Kristos's frustration.

Cruz popped the top off the glass bowl, which held a serving of chicken. Even cold, it smelled good. "Guess I'm hungrier than I thought." He looked down at Hubbard, who was licking his chops. "Relax, this one is all yours."

While the Westie ate, Cruz stretched out on his comforter. It didn't take long for Hubbard to lick his dish clean. Soon, the dog hopped onto the bed. Settling in beside Cruz, Hubbard laid his chin on Cruz's stomach. Two button eyes blinked at him, then closed.

Cruz stroked the petal-soft fur on Hubbard's head. "Cuddle time, huh? Looks like I can't go to dinner now," he whispered. He didn't mind.

Cruz's tablet on the nightstand was chiming. He put out an arm, his fingertips nudging the computer toward him until he could grab it. Cruz hit the video call icon. "Hi, Dad. Look who's here?" He tipped his screen toward a sleeping Hubbard.

"Aww. How's he doing?"

"Okay. I think he misses Taryn."

"I'm sure he does. How about you? How are *you* doing?"

"All right. We've been busy, so I haven't had a lot of time to think about . . . everything." Cruz told his dad about the animals he'd seen on their trek through the Kinabatangan River Basin, including the proboscis monkeys, orchid mantis, and exploding ants. He did not mention the tiger leech.

"Wow!" said his dad. "Your mom would have loved hearing about this."

He rubbed his chin. "So … um … have you … uh … made any progress on the clue?"

"No." Cruz knew his dad well enough to know that all those stops and starts meant he did not have good news. "You?"

"Sorry. I did another sweep of your room, but …"

"It's all right. It was a long shot."

"Keep trying," said his dad. "Something is bound to click. Where are you headed?"

"No idea. We're leaving port tomorrow, but no one is saying where we're going yet."

"Maybe Marisol will give you a hint?"

"I tried," grumbled Cruz. "She said I'd have to wait to find out with the rest of the explorers." He told his dad how everyone on his team had been guessing at their next destination. Bryndis thought it would be Japan; Dugan was betting Antarctica *(brrrr!)*; Lani said Thailand; Sailor, naturally, was keeping her fingers crossed for New Zealand; and Emmett had predicted China. "Emmett used an algorithm he'd designed based on curriculum records and navigational charts from all the ships in the Explorer Academy fleet over the past ten years," said Cruz.

"Sounds to me like you're going to China," chuckled his dad. "Where did you guess?"

"Where else? Hawaii!"

"I'm rooting for your choice, son. It's almost midnight here, so I'll say good night. Safe travels. Love you."

"Love you, too. Night, Dad."

Setting his tablet down on the bed, Cruz realized that this was one of the few times that they'd both been able to wish each other good night. Of course, it wasn't for the *same* night. Borneo was 18 hours ahead of Hanalei.

Cruz heard the muffled sound of a violin. Felipe was practicing next door. Note by note, his violin climbed the rungs of a musical ladder. It was like a lullaby, simple and soothing. Cruz snuggled Hubbard closer.

Fanchon would be coming in an hour or two to pick up the dog for the week ahead.

How could it be Sunday night already? Another week of not knowing the identity of Zebra or Jaguar. Another week of not solving his mom's clue. Had Prescott already figured it out? Cruz wondered. Did Nebula have a head start on him? And where was Roewyn? He hadn't heard anything from the daughter of the head of Nebula Pharmaceuticals since she'd surprised him at the Taj Mahal. Cruz hoped Roewyn was okay.

Cruz tugged on the lanyard around his neck until the stones tumbled into the hollow of his throat. Hooking his thumb around the cord, Cruz lifted it up and inspected the nearly complete circle of black marble dangling inches from his face. This *had* to be the extraordinary object his mom referred to in her journal. But what was ordinary about it? The marble? The shape? The engraving?

What?

What was he missing?

Hubbard's rhythmic breathing, Felipe's comforting scales, and the spinning cipher were making Cruz drowsy. No, he would not sleep until he figured out this mystery. His eyelids were heavy. His arm, too. The lanyard slipped from Cruz's thumb. He barely felt the stones land on his chest.

6

SOMETHING startled him. A noise, though Cruz couldn't say what.

He opened his eyes. He was still on top of his bed. Someone had placed a blanket over him, the spare one they always kept on the rack in the closet. The blinds were slightly open. Yet, no sunlight filtered through. Cruz's OS band read 10:46 p.m. He'd slept for more than four hours!

His friends must have decided not to disturb him when they'd returned from dinner. Apparently, nobody had solved the clue either or they would have woken him. Cruz patted the bed on both sides. Hubbard was gone. A turn of his head revealed the dog bed in the corner was empty, too. Fanchon must have been by to pick him up. Boy, he really must have been beat to sleep through it all.

Cruz heard rustling. A pair of light green glowing rings was hovering near Emmett's dresser—the emoto-frames. Emmett's feet must be cold again. Stretching his toes, Cruz waited for Emmett to grab his socks so that he could get up and put on his pajamas. No sense crashing into each other in the dark. Cruz watched Emmett pad past, but instead of getting into bed, his roommate opened the door and walked out of the cabin.

Was he still dreaming? He heard the latch click.

Cruz sat upright. What. Just. Happened? Emmett *never* broke the rules. And he sure never snuck out in the middle of the night. Did he?

There was only one person on board that Emmett would break curfew to see.

Cruz threw off the blanket and sprung out of bed. In the scramble to find his shoes, he stubbed his toe on the corner of the bed. "Ow!" He hobbled in a circle, trying to hop the pain away.

Mid-hop, Cruz stopped. Maybe this wasn't a good idea. If Emmett had wanted company, he would have said so, right? Besides, Dr. Lu might not come out of the secret Synthesis lab, or let Emmett in, if she spotted Cruz. He'd better stay. Cruz eased himself back down onto the corner of his mattress. What was Emmett up to? Could it be that his mom had some information about Dr. Fallowfeld? Is that why he'd snuck out? Yes! That had to be it. Cruz sighed. If only he could be a fly on the wall for *that* conversation . . .

Wait!

Cruz limped to his closet. Grabbing his jacket off its hook, Cruz shook it out and pressed his thumb against the honeycomb remote on his lapel. "Mell, on. Come to eye level, please." His honeybee drone flew out of his upper-right pocket. "Mell, follow Emmett. Send a live stream to my tablet," instructed Cruz. "Don't let him out of your sight but keep out of his, okay?"

Mell flashed her golden eyes twice.

"He's probably headed to B deck," said Cruz. "Mell, go!"

She zipped across the cabin, dropped down to slip through the space between the door and the floor, and was gone.

Cruz hit the bee icon on the screen of this tablet. From the menu, he brought up the live feed. It would allow him to see everything through Mell's eyes, as well as hear audio. He watched from Mell's vantage point as she flew down the explorers' passage, staying close to the ceiling. The corridor lights had been lowered for the night, but Mell had an excellent night-vision camera. Speeding into the atrium, she took a sharp left into the stairwell. The honeybee drone kept to the rail, but rather than continue down one more flight to B deck, she swerved into the passage of the main deck. Uh-oh! Where was Mell going? Had she forgotten his instructions?

Cruz put a hand to his remote to get the MAV back on course, when he saw two figures standing near the door to the gangway: Emmett and his mom. Their faces were partially lit by the lights from the pier. Or maybe it was the moon. In a red trench coat, Dr. Lu stood beside a rolling suitcase. Was she leaving the ship?

Mell landed on top of a brass lantern sconce on the opposite side of the corridor. She was about 10 feet away from Dr. Lu and Emmett.

"You shouldn't have come," said Dr. Lu, though her tone signaled she was glad he had. "If Nyomie finds out you've broken curfew..."

"I'll be okay. You know me," said Emmett, "always breaking the rules."

She laughed. So did Cruz.

"I'm sure going to miss sneaking out of the lab to have milk and cookies with you in the aquatics storage room," said Dr. Lu.

She *was* leaving. And the milk-and-cookies thing was news to Cruz.

"Me too." Emmett took a step toward his mom. "You're coming back, though, right?"

"No, hon."

Cruz's breath caught.

"But, Mom—"

"You've got everything you need," continued Dr. Lu. "Besides, it's time I return to headquarters. I have work to do. And so do you."

"Sure," said Emmett, though his head went back and forth, not up and down.

"Contact Jericho if you run into trouble," said Dr. Lu. "He'll know what to do."

"O-okay."

She put a hand on his arm. "You're doing fine."

"Only because you're here," muttered Emmett. "Now that you're going..."

"It has nothing to do with me, Nou-nou. It never did. *You* belong here. You always have. And it's time you discovered that for yourself."

"I guess." Emmett lifted a shoulder. "I just wish you were ..."

"Closer," whispered Cruz.

Emmett looked up at his mother. "Closer."

"I know." Dr. Lu put her arms around him. Emmett hugged his mother. As he leaned his head against her shoulder, a beam of light from the pier lit his face. Emmett closed his eyes. The emoto-glasses turned raspberry pink.

Cruz felt a lump in his throat.

Dr. Lu released her son. She reached for her suitcase and, with one last wave, stepped through the opening in the hull. Due to Mell's sharp angle, she was soon out of Cruz's sight, though he could hear the wheels of the suitcase bump-ing down the metal ramp. Emmett raised his hand, his fingers slowly curling closed.

The sound of wheels fading, Emmett dropped his hand. A moment later, he walked back down the passage, strolling past the lantern sconce where Mell sat. The bee drone stayed put, moving only her head to track Emmett as he became a shadowy figure in the dimness. Cruz was about to shut off the live stream when his roommate stopped.

Emmett's silhouette may have been hazy, but his voice was clear. "Coming, Mell?"

SWIRLING MAPLE SYRUP TO THE CRISPY GOLDEN corners of his French toast, Cruz felt a tremor. Next to him, Bryndis's fingers had stopped peeling the shell from her hard-boiled egg. She'd felt it, too.

"We're moving!" Sailor spun to peer out the dining room window. "Goodbye, Borneo."

"Goodbye, proboscis monkeys," said Emmett.

Dugan was drowning everything on his plate—pancakes, eggs, even diced potatoes—in syrup. "Goodbye, Ali's moth."

"I wonder which one of us will win the bet on our destination?" laughed Lani.

Cruz had a feeling they wouldn't have to wait long for the answer. And he was right.

Entering Manatee classroom, they were greeted by an enthusiastic Professor Luben, as usual. "Good morning, explorers! I trust you're all rested and refreshed from our recent mission."

"Yep," clipped Dugan. As he took his seat, Dugan shot Cruz a mischievous look. "How about you, Professor Luben? Do anything *fun* yesterday?"

Sailor kicked the back of Dugan's chair.

Fortunately, their teacher missed Dugan's meaning. Instead, he told them about how he'd played the new ATV game in the CAVE, beating Monsieur Legrand two out of three games. "All right, let's get started. We have a lot to cover today." Professor Luben rubbed his hands together the way he always did when he was excited. "I'm sure it hasn't escaped your notice that we've put to sea. You must be curious about our destination. The rest of the faculty has informed me that at this point in the year the standard curriculum for first-year recruits would have us sailing to China—"

The rest of his sentence was lost in an explosion of applause.

"Giant pandas!" hooted Matteo.

"The Great Wall!" cried Zane.

"Clouded leopards," sighed Lani.

Emmett leaned back, placing his hands behind his head in triumph. He'd won Team Cousteau's bet, as its members knew he would.

Professor Luben's mouth was drawn into a straight line, and the explorers quickly settled. "As I was saying," their teacher continued, "our travels *would* have taken us to China, but recent events have caused us to alter course."

Recent events? Alter course? What did he mean?

"Dim lights to twenty percent, please," ordered their teacher.

As the classroom lights went down, Professor Luben stepped to one side. A second later, a holo-video of an animal appeared where he'd been standing. It looked like a cross between a wild dog, a tiger, and a kangaroo. It had the short, rounded ears, large eyes, and snout of a wolf. Yet its body looked more like a greyhound's, strong yet streamlined. Thick black stripes cut across the short, sand-colored fur on its back, leading to a long, tapered tail.

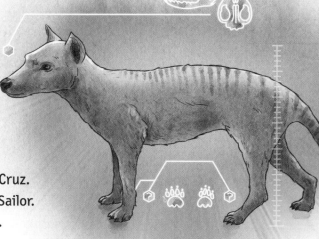

"What is it?" whispered Cruz.

"A thylacine," answered Sailor.

Dugan swung in his seat.

"A what-a-sign?"

"Meet the thylacine," said Professor Luben. "It's also known as the Tasmanian tiger or Tasmanian wolf. However, it's not a cat or dog. It's a carnivorous marsupial, a relative of the numbat, Tasmanian devil, and quoll."

A short, rounded ear twitched, almost as if the animal were listening to Professor Luben's talk. The thylacine put its black nose up, sniffing into the wind. While they watched, it turned its head and a pair of wide, dark doe eyes looked directly at them. It was kind of cute.

"Awwww," cooed Ali.

The thylacine opened its mouth, and Ali nearly toppled out of his seat. "Whoa!"

"It has jaws like an alligator!" cried Dugan.

"With that whopping gape it does look quite vicious, doesn't it?" said their teacher. "The truth is, the thylacine is actually a timid nocturnal creature. Here's another fun fact: The female has a pouch where she may carry up to four joeys, though the pouch faces the hind legs rather than the head the way a kangaroo's does—"

"Professor Luben?" Sailor's arm was in the air. "I don't mean to correct you, but you keep saying 'is' and 'has.' Shouldn't it be 'was' and 'had'? The thylacine went extinct like a hundred years ago."

Professor Luben paused the holo-video. "Explorers, what I am about to reveal to you is confidential information. You cannot share it with anyone other than your teachers, Fanchon Quills, Sidril Vanderwick, and Dr. Eikenboom. You can't discuss it with friends, family, or even *Orion*'s crew, who know where we're going but don't know why. Do you understand?"

"Yes," 24 explorers answered as one.

"Please raise your hand if you agree to abide by these rules."

Twenty-four hands shot up.

"Good," said their teacher. "The holo-video that you've been viewing was recorded in the southern region of the Australian island of Tasmania. However, it's not archival footage from a century or more ago. This"— Professor Luben glanced at the thylacine frozen in midair—"was taken five weeks ago."

Everyone gasped.

Except Sailor. She let out a "Phhht," earning her a raised eyebrow from their teacher. "Sailor, do you have something to contribute?" he asked.

"Sorry. I don't mean to be rude and you couldn't know because you're not from down under, but the thylacine is . . . well, it's become a legend," said Sailor. "You know, like the Loch Ness monster or Bigfoot? See, every couple of years, somebody walks out of a Tassie forest saying they've spotted a thylacine so they can get on the news or write a book or whatever. The photos and videos *always* turn out to be fake." She pointed to the holo-image. "This one looks real, to be sure, but I wouldn't get your hopes up. It's probably another hoax."

"You can't compare this to Nessie and Bigfoot," said Yulia. "I mean, those *were* legends. They never existed in the first place. But we *know* the thylacine was real. It's possible it's still out there."

Sailor started to open her mouth, but Matteo, Yulia's Magellan teammate, said, "Besides, how can we ignore this? Come on, Sailor, where's your spirit of adventure? Don't be such a . . . I don't know how to say it in English . . . a stick figure."

That got a few snickers.

"I think you mean stick-in-the-mud," said Ali. "But we get it."

Nobody from Team Cousteau cracked a smile. Sailor's cheeks went pink. Cruz couldn't tell if it was from embarrassment or anger. He knew that although the insult seemed minor, it cut deep. No explorer wanted to be thought of as wimpy or scared, least of all Sailor. Cruz wasn't sure what was going through Sailor's mind, but he knew how he felt. Mad. He dug his fingers into the cushion of his chair, wondering if he should he speak up and defend his friend.

"Hold on, class," said their teacher. "Sailor is smart to be skeptical."

Cruz relaxed his grip. *Thank you, Professor Luben!*

"At this point in my lecture, as explorers, you should have more questions than answers," said their teacher firmly. "You don't know where this footage originated, if it's been authenticated by experts, or been confirmed by any other scientific means—all reasons to be cautious." He grinned at Sailor, who sat up a little taller. "Here is what we know: This video is from a dragonfly drone. It came from a young Society scientist doing research on bird migration, and it has been seen by two of our most experienced Australian wildlife biologists. They believe it is the real deal but, like Sailor, they have doubts, too. They need more data." Their professor opened his arms. "And that is where you come in. Explorers, your next mission will be to help determine if the thylacine, an animal that we thought was long gone from the Earth, still exists."

An excited murmur went through the room.

"As you know, one of the best ways to discover the habits of animals is through camera trap technology," said their professor. "Remote cameras can travel to and remain in the most extreme and remote areas of the globe, from the coldest regions of Antarctica to the hottest deserts in Africa to the deepest parts of the ocean. Your mission will take you into the Tasmania wilderness to deploy Fanchon's SHOT-bots in the area where this video was taken. We're hoping that one or more of these traveling, motion-activated camera traps will capture video of the elusive thylacine."

Professor Luben brought the lights up. "It will take *Orion* roughly ten days to reach Tasmania, so we'll be using some of our class time to prepare you. Professor Ishikawa will teach you about the biology of the animal, Professor Coronado will cover the fossil record, Professor Benedict will provide historical elements and help you hone your observation and photography skills, Monsieur Legrand will boost your endurance for the long trek into the forest, and so on. Questions? Yes, Lani?"

"If we can prove that the thylacine exists, what then?"

"We're hopeful the SHOT-bots will do more than provide video of the thylacine," said Professor Luben. "They may be able to reveal some information about population size and behaviors, such as hunting, feeding, mating, and how the animals raise their young. It also might be possible to actually locate one of the marsupials to take measurements, get samples, and attach a tracking collar. This would be well down the line, mind you."

"S-samples?" sputtered Cruz. "You mean, as in hair and saliva?"

"Blood, too," said Professor Luben.

Cruz's mind was racing. "That means we would have its DNA . . . and . . . and with its genetic code, science could clone it—I mean, if it was close to extinction."

Their teacher was strolling his way. "That's correct."

"So, what you're saying is"—Cruz's heart was suddenly pounding so hard he could barely hear himself speak—"if the thylacine is really out there, the future of the species could depend on . . . well . . . *us*."

Towering over him, Professor Luben scratched his stubbled jaw. It sounded like sandpaper. "Yes, Cruz. It very well could."

7

IN EVERY CLASS, the explorers' teachers were eager to talk about their mission to Tasmania. Aunt Marisol showed them thylacine fossils that were more than two million years old, explaining that some of the earliest types of the species dated back more than 20 million years! In her class, they also viewed photos of pictographs—rock paintings of the thylacine that ancient Aboriginals had done several thousands of years earlier when the marsupial once roamed the Australian mainland.

Professor Ishikawa told them that the thylacine's Latin name, *Thylacinus cynocephalus,* translated to "pouched dog with a wolf's head." Even so, evidence indicated that it ambushed its prey the way a cat does, rather than chasing it like a dog. Their biology teacher told them thylacines typically hunted wombats, kangaroos, rodents, and birds.

"When we're in the woods, will we be able to spot thylacine tracks?" asked Bryndis.

"Unfortunately, we don't have a distinct thylacine print to go by," said their professor. "The only footprints on record are those taken from museum samples a century ago, not actual paw prints from the ground. We don't know important details like how far apart the digital pads are, what the metacarpal print might look like, or the length of the animal's gait. Some researchers have made guesses, but that's not good enough. Science requires evidence. If the SHOT-bots do their jobs, maybe one day, Bryndis, we'll be able to recognize their tracks."

In journalism class, the explorers read newspaper articles about how the thylacine was widespread in Tasmania in the early 1800s, but as Europeans settled the area, they viewed the thylacine as predators of their livestock, even though the animal rarely preyed on sheep or chickens. To reduce thylacine populations, the government and land-owners placed a bounty on the animal. By the early 19th century, between being hunted and losing their habitat, thylacines were a rare sight in Tasmania. "By the time people started realizing they were wip-ing out the species, it was too late," explained Professor Benedict, as they watched a black-and-white video of a thylacine pacing in a cage. "In 1936, less than two months after laws were passed to protect the animal, this thylacine—the last one known to be alive at the time—died in a zoo in the Tasmanian capital of Hobart."

Seeing the animal nervously trot back and forth in the enclosure was heartbreaking. Some of the explorers—Ali, Tao, Blessica, Matteo—looked away. Cruz did not. As unsettling as the video was, he knew he needed to watch it. He also wanted to memorize the animal in as much detail as possible. His teammates were doing the same.

Less than two minutes after Professor Benedict had dismissed them for the day, Cruz's comm pin crackled with the voice of their tech lab chief.

"Do you have a minute?" asked Fanchon. "I need to speak with you."

"Uh … sure. Class just let out. Do you want me to come to the tech lab?"

"As soon as possible."

"I'll be right there." Signing off, he caught Lani's frown. "She sounded pretty serious, didn't she? You don't think she's mad that I fell asleep last night and she had to come get Hubbard, do you?"

"That doesn't sound like Fanchon, but maybe. You'd better apologize."

With a quick wave, Cruz flew up the stairs to the fourth deck.

Fanchon, wearing a turquoise-and-green tie-dyed head scarf with a school of bright yellow tang circling it, was waiting for him inside the tech lab. She was also clutching a tablet, one of the larger ones that Dr. Vanderwick often used. On the front of her pale blue apron was an illustration of a cell holding up a camera with the words *Cell-fie* printed below it. Cruz snickered. Fanchon, however, did not break into her usual easy grin. There were shadows under her eyes. "I'm sorry about Hubbard," said Cruz.

Her brow wrinkled. "Hubbard?"

"About falling asleep last night and not bringing him to you."

"Oh … right. No problem. I didn't mind coming to get him." She heard a drawer shut, and her eyes darted around. "We can't talk here," whispered Fanchon. "Come with me." Spinning, she scurried into the labyrinth of cubicles. Cruz stayed on her heels as she zigzagged through the maze like a hungry mouse on the trail of a hunk of cheese. What was going on? he wondered.

Reaching the back wall of the lab, Fanchon stopped in front of a black door marked TECH STAFF ONLY. She punched a code into the keypad next to the door: 4-2-9-2-4-4. Cruz heard whirring. It sounded like a microwave cooking food. A blue ray shot out of the iris scanner, and Fanchon leaned to stare into it.

Cruz felt his heart stutter. Seriously? Was she really taking him into the Super-Secret Room? Rumor was that this was the place where Fanchon kept her most important and confidential experiments and inventions. The head of the tech lab always told them that anything was possible, so Cruz had let his imagination run wild about what the room contained. If anything *was* possible, Cruz could invent a device that let him read other people's minds, or maybe a time-traveling potion or a car that could transport you at the speed of light or—

"Cruz?" Fanchon was motioning for him to go through the open door.

Stepping over the threshold, he saw a seam in the floor. There were actually two doors for each side of the room, like in some elevators. Fanchon followed him in, and both doors shut.

To his left, Cruz saw a row of upper and lower black cabinets separated by a long black counter. To his right, same thing. Cruz glimpsed doors and drawers bearing labels like TONGS, GRADUATED CYLINDERS, and BEAKERS. This was it? A storage room? Not even a single petri dish of orange sensotivia gel? Talk about a letdown.

Fanchon caught his expression. "Sorry to disappoint you. It's not the inner sanctum. We're in lab three."

"Huh?"

"It's part of a revolving compartment. See, I can choose from three different rooms. I key in a code at the pad to select which one I want and that room rotates to the door in the main lab that we just came through. The technical term is a gyroscopic laboratory, but Sidril and I nicknamed it the merry-go-lab."

"Wow!" Cruz wondered how many people knew about this.

"This is the only room I can let you see," explained Fanchon. "It's secure and soundproof. I had to be sure we wouldn't be disturbed or overhead."

Whatever she wanted to talk about, it must be important for her to bring him here. "What's going on?" Cruz's voice cracked with worry.

"It involves your mom's logbook."

"Oh." Another wave of disappointment washed over Cruz. Fanchon had probably recovered more of the page from his PANDA unit. He appreciated it, but it was of no use to him now. Thanks to his visit to the Archive, he'd read the complete entry. He couldn't tell her that, of course. "What I mean is ... that's great." Cruz didn't want to hurt her feelings. "Were you able to reveal more of the entry?"

"No, unfortunately. I went as far as I could with that, but I did manage to get something else ..." Tapping her screen, Fanchon tilted the big tablet toward him. Cruz watched the video of his mother reading her logbook captured by the PANDA he'd seen many times. However, instead of ending in a freeze frame, as it had before, Cruz saw his mother lift her hand and ...

Turn the page!

Cruz couldn't believe it. "How…how…?"

"Watch," ordered Fanchon. "It goes by fast."

On the fresh page, Cruz caught a glimpse of two words: *Tardinia Serum*. Below the title was part of an equation. He bent for a closer look only to see his mother tear that page, along with several others, out of the logbook. She slammed the cover shut. The screen went black.

"Nooooo!" cried Cruz. The formula! It had been right there, for a brief second, anyway. "Fanchon, back it up so we can see—"

"Already did. The equation is part of a dosage calculation. Helpful if we ever learn the components of the serum but until then useless. *However*…" Fanchon began typing again.

No wonder the Synthesis had only let Cruz see one page of his mother's notebook. The Synthesis didn't have the cell-regeneration formula—they had *never* had it! That's why Jericho Miles was on *Orion*. The Synthesis was waiting for Cruz to complete the cipher. They needed him! The big question was, once Cruz had uncovered all eight stones, what would the Synthesis do? Protect him? Or force him to turn it over to them?

"Remember how I told you I'd read nearly every paper, essay, and article your mom ever wrote?" asked Fanchon. "'Tardinia' sounded familiar, but I couldn't place where I'd seen it. I went back through some old Society professional journals and found this article your mom wrote a decade ago." Fanchon spun her tablet. "Look! She discussed the potential of using animal venoms in cell regeneration. She said the right formulation could lead to humans being born with the ability to fight off almost any disease. She compared it to the tardigrade."

"Tardigrades? We learned about them in biology," said Cruz, recalling the teeny water-dwellers that, under the microscope, resembled transparent, eight-legged caterpillars. "Professor Ishikawa says they're tiny but mighty."

"That's true." Fanchon nodded. "They're resilient, all right. You can freeze them, boil them, smash them, withhold food and water, even zap them with radiation and they won't die—"

"We read that they orbited Earth on the *outside* of a rocket," said Cruz.

"They *can* live in space. Plus, they've survived all of Earth's mass extinctions. Tardigrades can wait out extreme cold and drought by dehydrating and then rehydrate ten or twenty *years* later once environmental conditions improve," said Fanchon. "They're practically immortal!"

Goose bumps skittered down Cruz's arms.

Fanchon set her tablet on the counter. "You want to know what I think?"

Did he?

She didn't wait for his answer. "I think your mom developed a cell-regeneration formula she named Tardinia. I think, somehow, she exposed herself and you to that formula. I think she ripped some critical pages out of her scientific logbook before she died, and I think you know something about why she did it."

Cruz slapped his chest and feigned confusion. "Me? Huh-uh. No way—"

"'When I handled the serum, I didn't notice the cut on my hand . . . I am unsure, but I know I must find a way.'" Fanchon was quoting from his mom's logbook. "'How do you begin to tell your son his destiny may be …?'" The yellow tang on her head scarf swam close. Dark eyes searched his. Fanchon Quills was waiting for Cruz to finish her sentence, but how could he? He'd made a promise. He was not allowed to say the three words he knew came next: *to live forever.*

An icy shudder rippled down his spine as a realization hit. Is that why Fanchon had brought him to this soundproof room? To get the truth out of him before she killed him? There was nowhere to go, no one to hear him call for help. Cruz was trapped.

Fanchon was Zebra!

It was his own fault. He should have been more careful. Cruz slid his right hand into his pocket, closing it around the octopod. Funny. He was about to use the very weapon Fanchon had made for him *on her.* Even so, before he activated it, he'd need an escape route or he'd be a victim of the paralytic spray, too.

"What do you want?" asked Cruz, trying to stall for time, as his eyes darted here and there.

"What do you think? For you to trust me, of course." Fanchon stepped back. "But you don't, and I can't blame you."

This was not the reaction he'd expected.

She tugged at the top of her apron, pulling it up to her chin as if it were a shell she wanted to hide in. "I wish I could undo what happened with the Universal Cetacean Communicator. If only you could erase your mistakes like words on a page, but you can't, can you? Cruz, you *have* to believe me. I ran the helmet through every possible test, and it passed with flying colors. I would never have sent you down there with it if I thought for one second it could, or would, be sabotaged."

Cruz relaxed his grip on the octopod. "I know that, Fanchon. I know that what happened with the UCC helmet wasn't your fault. I don't blame you, really, I don't." He wanted to add that he trusted her, but did he? "Thanks for advancing the logbook. Honestly, you know more about the serum than I do. I … I don't know why Mom ripped the page out of her book. I'm sorry."

The lies were getting harder to tell.

"Okay. Thanks anyway." She was disappointed. "We'd better get back." Moving past him, Fanchon pressed the button to open the doors. When they didn't slide open, Fanchon tried again. Still, the doors didn't budge. She tapped her comm pin. "Fanchon Quills to Sidril Van—Oh!"

The ship suddenly shifted. The jolt threw Fanchon into Cruz, hurling them both backward into the end of the lower cabinets.

"Hold on!" shouted Fanchon.

Cruz's first thought, as he fell to his knees and hugged the corner of the cabinets, was that *Orion* had been slammed by a giant wave. Yet the ship was still upright. A collision? But they were still moving. What was going on? The force of motion was pushing Cruz into the cabinets. That's when he realized the room was turning counterclockwise. "Fanchon, someone's running the merry-go-lab!" he called.

"They can't." Fanchon was above him, her arms spread wide as she clung to the top of the counter. "It has a safety shut-off feature. The wheel mechanism automatically locks down when anyone is in one of the labs so no one can get trapped or caught in the rotation."

"You mean like we are right now?" Cruz's teeth were rattling.

"It must be a malfunction," said Fanchon. "I bet Sidril needed to use one of the labs. I didn't tell her I was coming in. Hang tight. It'll stop in a minute." She hit her comm pin again. "Fanchon to Sidril Vanderwick."

Her assistant didn't respond. And the room didn't stop spinning. In fact, it was picking up speed. Cruz was starting to get dizzy. He was also regretting having a spicy beef burrito wrap with guacamole for lunch. Trying to readjust, Fanchon's hand slipped off the counter. Cruz heard a sharp crack a second before he saw her crumple to the floor next to the wall.

"Fanchon!"

She didn't move. Cruz tried to get up but couldn't get his feet under him on the slick floor. Stumbling, he hit his knee on the cabin and went down. Pain shot down his leg. Cruz grabbed a drawer pull with one hand and hit his comm pin with the other. "Cruz to Marisol

Coronado. Need ... help ... tech lab ... gyro ... room three ..."

He got no response.

Cruz knew if he let go of the drawer, like Fanchon, he would be flung into the wall with a force violent enough to break bones. Or worse. Spinning like a Frisbee in a windstorm was beginning to scramble his brain. His thoughts were becoming jumbled. Everything was a blur. His ears hurt. His stomach churned.

Sick and dizzy, Cruz didn't know how much longer he could hold on. He was going to pass out. The merry-go-lab was going faster and faster and faster ...

8

THE PINK SOLES of Fanchon's shoes were going in and out of focus. Cruz knew he had to do something, and fast, before he lost consciousness, too.

Turning onto his hip, Cruz pressed his palm into the honeycomb pin on his chest. "Mell, on! Come to eye level." He felt the brush of her wings against his neck as she rocketed out of his pocket. "Fly into the control panel! See if you can short-circuit it or something ... stop the room from rotating. Mell, go!" Cruz thought he saw her golden eyes flash twice, but everything was in motion, so who knew?

Cruz closed his eyes. He slowed his breathing and told himself to stay calm. He hoped Fanchon wasn't badly hurt. Cruz wanted to check on her, but with the merry-go-lab whirling like a top, there was no way. If Emmett were here, he'd probably be calculating the centrifugal force. Cruz would be satisfied if he could just keep his lunch down.

It took Cruz a moment to realize that his body was no longer being jammed against the cabinets. His stomach was settling. Could it be ...?

He opened his eyes. The lab was slowing! *Yay, Mell!*

Cruz lifted his head. The room was still revolving, but they were traveling much slower—less than half the speed of before, he guessed. Moving at this rate, Cruz was pretty sure he could stand and balance the way he did on his surfboard, but walk? That might be tricky. Uncurling his fingers from the drawer pull, Cruz began to crawl across the shiny black floor. His chest against tile, arms and legs moving like a frog through shallow waters, he wriggled his way toward the tech lab chief. Cruz reached for her foot. "Fanchon?"

She moaned.

Cruz let out a relieved sigh as he scooted up to her shoulder. "You all right?"

"I...I think so." She winced. "Are we still spinning, or is it me?"

"We're spinning, all right, but Mell was able to get into the circuitry and slow us down."

Bzzz! Bzzz!

Cruz glanced up. Blinking once, the honeybee shook her head. She hadn't been able to complete her shut-down mission. "It's okay, Mell," said Cruz. "Every bit helps."

"Let's see if we can get some more help," said Fanchon. She tried again to raise Dr. Vanderwick on the comm link. Cruz tried to contact his aunt and Emmett. Nobody answered.

"Our comms should be working, even if the lab isn't," said Fanchon.

Unless someone doesn't want us getting out of here, thought Cruz.

"I'm on the wrong side." Fanchon pushed herself up to sit against the wall. "If only I wasn't *in* here, I could figure out a way to stop this thing."

"Maybe we don't have to." Cruz was getting an idea. "Stop it, I mean."

"Huh?"

"Didn't you ever jump off a merry-go-round when you were a kid?"

"Sure, but I'm no kid and this is no merry-go-round," clipped the tech lab chief. "We're not aiming for the ground, Cruz. We'd have to jump *through* the doorway into the main lab. That's a pretty small target to hit."

"I know, but—"

"If we timed it wrong, if we went a fraction of a second too early or too late, we'd hit the wall—splat! Like a bug on a windshield." Fanchon looked up. "No offense, Mell."

Mell tipped her head as if to say, *None taken.*

"Then we won't miss," said Cruz.

"More like we *can't* miss." Fanchon rubbed her head. "Let's take it one step at a time. First, let's see if Mell can even open the set of doors. If they wouldn't open for me—"

"She'll do it," said Cruz. He gave the MAV her instructions. With a double flash of her golden eyes, the drone sped away.

"Let's get over to the doorway," said Fanchon. "If Mell succeeds, we might be able to get Sidril's attention as we pass the main lab, if she's near the doors."

"Still too chicken to jump?"

"Bok-bok-bok," she clucked.

On hands and knees, they worked their way over to the corner closest to the door. Cruz leaned against the wall, walking his hands up it until he was back on his feet. He turned and put his right foot in front of him and his left foot in back, in goofy foot position, as if waiting for a wave to break. Cruz slowly windmilled his arms for balance. "Just like back home." He grinned at the tech lab chief. "Have you ever surfed?"

The yellow fish on Fanchon's head scarf swam back and forth.

"Watch me." Once he was steady, Cruz held out a hand to Fanchon. She took it, then carefully stood, sliding her right foot forward and bending her knees, copying Cruz.

Whooooosh!

They felt a breeze. A curved wall was rushing past. The bee had done it!

"There it is!" cried Cruz as they sailed by the opening to the main lab. "That door is open, too."

"Do you see Sidril?"

"No," he said. "But we went by pretty fast. Let's check again next pass."

The merry-go-lab circled past the main lab several times. Each time it did, Fanchon and Cruz looked for Dr. Vanderwick. They shouted her name. No one came.

"Looks like we'll have to go with your plan, Cruz," said Fanchon, inching toward the doorway. "Wish me luck."

"You?" croaked Cruz as Mell came in for a landing on his shoulder. "You're going to be the one to jump? It should be me."

"You may be the better athlete, but I'm the one that can stop this compartment. I think. Besides, if you got hurt—"

"I won't."

"I'm not willing to take that chance. This is no time to argue, Cruz. I've made my decision." Fanchon glanced at the MAV. "Mell, calculate the distance the merry-go-lab is traveling and the speed per revolution, factoring in the size of the opening to the main lab. I'm going to need for you to tell me when to leap."

Bzzz! confirmed Mell.

Cruz also had the drone take a quick video of what was happening. In the event Fanchon was injured in her attempt, Mell was to find Dr. Vanderwick and play the recording. Acknowledging Cruz's commands, the bee flitted to Fanchon's head scarf.

"Mell's ready," Cruz told Fanchon. "When you hear her buzz, go."

"Okay." Fanchon gulped. Her eyes were the size of quarters.

"You can do it," said Cruz. "Put one leg in front like you're hopping lily pads, okay? Then, once you land, tuck and roll. You don't want to break your ankle."

"Got it." Fanchon raised her arms.

Cruz kept his eyes on the curved wall. He released Fanchon's fingers but held his hand close in case she needed him to steady her. Mell had worked her way down Fanchon's head until she was a few inches above the lab chief's right ear. "Get ready, Fanchon!" he called.

"You know, I ran hurdles in high school, but that was a long time ago." Fanchon's voice trembled. "And I only did it because Cozette Autry was sick and I didn't want to let the team down—"

Bzzzzzz!

Fanchon was airborne! Caramel curls, a billowing apron, and pink shoes flew across the gap. It was a good leap. Her agility surprised

Cruz. She had great reflexes, all right, but had she made it? Cruz would have to wait until he came around again to know for sure.

He held his breath, as the compartment continued its rotation. It seemed to take forever, but finally, the doorway to the main lab came into view ...

There she was! Fanchon was in the lab, waving both arms. She didn't appear hurt, thank goodness! She yelled something about shutting down the lab. Cruz nodded and hung on.

And circled.

And circled.

And circled.

On the sixth revolution, Fanchon was shaking her head. "I can't ... It won't ..."

He didn't hear the rest of it, but he didn't have to. Something was clearly wrong. She couldn't stop the merry-go-lab. Cruz was going to have to jump, too. He'd instructed Mell to stay with Fanchon, so he would have to make his best guess on when to go.

Cruz got into his stance, holding the sides of the doorway. He filled his lungs and relaxed his grip on the doorjamb. Out of the corner of his eye, Cruz could see the entrance to the main lab coming up. Not yet ... not yet ...

Cruz felt a stabbing pain in his left wrist.

Now!

He flew across the divide. Cruz led with his shoulder, tucked his head, and braced for impact. He smashed into the unforgiving floor, clamping his eyes shut a second before every ounce of air was forced from his lungs. Cruz bounced along the tiled floor, trying to keep himself in as tight a ball as possible. He felt his foot jerk. Someone had grabbed on to him to help him brake. Cruz skidded to a stop next to a cubicle wall. Gasping, he opened his eyes to see Dr. Vanderwick and Mell above him. Was he still in one piece?

"You did it!" cried Dr. Vanderwick. "Are you hurt?"

On his side, Cruz unfolded himself. "I don't think so." Even if he was injured, Cruz knew it wouldn't take him long to heal. "What happened? Fanchon was going to shut it down from here."

"We can't get our controls to respond," said Dr. Vanderwick. "Comms are down, too. Fanchon is on her way to the main breaker in the engine room."

Cruz's wrist was sore. "Was that...? Did Mell sting me?"

"Probably. We sent her back for you. She didn't want to go, but Fanchon told her that she outranked you." She chuckled. "Guess the bee must not have had enough time to get within earshot to buzz at you."

"Mell!" Cruz tried to sound the way his father did when he was disappointed in him but not truly angry.

Mell lifted her wings as if to say, *Sorry.* However, by the way she was wiggling her antennas, Cruz got the feeling she got a kick out of stinging him. Nice.

Cruz rolled onto his back and let out a deep belly laugh. It was due in part to shock, but mostly it was relief. He'd taken a wild ride on the carousel of death and, somehow, had survived. Catching his breath, Cruz rested a warm cheek against the cool floor and enjoyed the comforting hum of *Orion*'s engines. Peace. Silence. Stillness. He drank it in. Filling and draining air from his lungs felt good.

What had he been thinking? Cruz never should have doubted Fanchon. She *was* right: After the accident with the UCC, he *had* been wary of her. He had not realized how the incident still haunted her until she'd said she longed to forget the past—no, that wasn't right. Erase the past. That was what she'd said. Like words on a page.

Cruz heard his mom's voice. *Something others use to forget the past will reveal your future.*

Staring at the wall of the tech lab, Cruz wondered, could the solution be that simple? It *was* in her box of things: the only item that could, literally, allow you to undo the past. Is that what his mom wanted him to use on the pages she'd wrapped around the stones? Would the secret message then be revealed? Maybe. He was afraid to hope again. But maybe.

A tiny sparkle caught Cruz's eye.

It had been swept into a crevice between the tiles directly under the merry-go-lab control panel. It was luck, really, that he'd even seen it at all. Had he not been lying on the floor with his head turned just so, it's unlikely Cruz would ever have spotted the little silk daisy with a yellow jewel in its center. But he was. And he did.

CRUZ SWUNG OPEN THE DOOR of his cabin to find Emmett, Sailor, and Lani huddled over his desk.

"There you are! We've been trying to reach you, but comms are off-line." Sailor started toward him. "Lani thinks that—whoa! You look carked. Are you sick? Need to chunder?" She stepped aside to clear a path to the bathroom.

"No plans to toss my cookies now, but ten minutes ago—" Cruz saw that his mom's box was sitting on the corner of his desk. The lid was on.

"We were getting it ready for when you got back," burst Lani. "We wouldn't have opened it without your permission, Cruz. Honest."

"I know. It's all right." Cruz went to his desk. "You guys can look in it anytime you want. We're a team, remember? Besides, I think I know why you're here." He lifted the lid and fished around until he found what he was looking for. Cruz held up the eraser.

"You got unstuck," said Lani. "I knew you would."

Cruz stretched out his hand to her. "Want to see if we're right?"

"Really?"

"You *were* here first. It's only fair." Plus, he was still a bit shaky from his ride on the merry-go-lab. He didn't want to damage the paper.

Lani took the pink wedge and settled into the desk chair. Cruz brought her the two pages of aqua parchment from his nightstand. Sailor moved to Lani's left and smoothed down the first page. Emmett went around to Lani's right and did the same with the other page. Cruz stood behind them, clasping his hands and chewing on his thumbnail.

"Here goes." Starting at the top-left corner of the first page, Lani began erasing . . . well, nothing. Using long, careful strokes, she moved the eraser across the width of the paper from left to right. When she reached the end of the invisible row, she dropped the eraser down a bit and began again. Cruz saw only pink flecks in her wake. By the fifth line, it was pretty obvious what was happening. Nothing. Nothing was happening—no message, no code, no map, no new clue.

Cruz turned away. Raising his arms out from his sides, he flopped face-first onto his bed. His limp body bounced a few times. Cruz let his face sink into the pillow. What was he supposed to do now?

"She's got something!" cried Emmett.

Cruz sprang off his bed. Peering over Lani's shoulder, he watched a series of numbers magically appear on the page: 34.3841° N, 109.2785° E.

GPS coordinates!

"I'm on it!" Sailor scrambled for her tablet.

Finishing the first page, Lani moved on to the second piece of parchment. She had only to rub across the paper once before something appeared. It was a photograph! Cruz saw dark gray. Stone? Yes! And round. A head. A stone head!

Under Lani's hand, the secrets of the page were gradually revealed: hair pulled up into a topknot, arched eyebrows, carved eyes with no pupils, a well-trimmed mustache curling past the corners of an unsmiling mouth, an upside-down triangle of a beard tucked beneath a lower lip.

As Lani continued working down the page, Cruz saw a thick rolled turtleneck and an overlay of armor. Bulging rivets attached the dozens of small overlapping squares that covered his shoulders and the entire front of his body. Around his neck, the man wore a chain that held a medallion with a dark red stone. In a picture of drab and dusty grays, Cruz's eye was immediately drawn to the smooth scarlet oval resting over the man's heart. The statue's right elbow was bent, his hand curled as if it had once held something between his thumb and finger. To the warrior's left, right, and behind him were similar soldiers, so many that they went beyond the camera's depth of field and became a blur. The warriors stood between the high dirt walls of a trench in perfect formation. All stared straight ahead.

Cruz instantly knew this archaeological wonder. "The Terra-Cotta Army," he whispered.

"Got it!" exclaimed Sailor. "The coordinates lead to the Emperor Qin Shi Huang Di Mausoleum and the Museum of the Terra-Cotta Warriors and Horses. It's east of Xi'an, the capital city of Shaanxi Province."

Cruz rested a hand on Lani's shoulder. "Looks like we're going to China after all."

She grinned up at him.

There was a knock at the door. Everybody froze.

"Our comms must still be down," whispered Emmett. "It's probably Dugan or Bryndis to go to dinner."

Cruz put a finger to his lips. If they stayed still, whoever it was would go away.

Five seconds later, another knock. "Cruz? Emmett?"

Aunt Marisol! Panic bubbled within Cruz. His hand went to the jacket pocket that held a small silk daisy. He'd swept the white fake flower into his palm when Fanchon wasn't looking. Cruz needed to know if it belonged to his aunt. And if it *did*, what then? What did it prove? Only that Aunt Marisol had been in the lab between the time he'd met her on the grand staircase yesterday and this afternoon. It didn't mean she had sabotaged the merry-go-lab—if what had occurred *was* sabotage.

Cruz's heart was thumping. His airway tightened. He knew he shouldn't rush to judgment, but how could he stay calm? Cruz tried to shake it out of his mind, but like a quarter stuck in a piggy bank it refused to fall. He *had* to know.

Was Aunt Marisol Zebra?

9

FEARFUL brown eyes zeroed in on Cruz. "Are you all right?"

"Yep."

"When I heard that the gyroscopic lab went crazy and you were inside—"

"I'm okay, Aunt Marisol," insisted Cruz.

Sailor's head was bouncing between Cruz and his aunt. She'd opened the door. "What's a gyroscopic lab?" she directed to Aunt Marisol, then to Cruz, "And what happened to you in it?"

"It's a revolving compartment with a trio of rooms within the tech lab," explained Emmett. "It's where Fanchon and Dr. Vanderwick keep their most sensitive and secret experiments. They call it the merry-go-lab 'cause, you know, it rotates."

Cruz couldn't help smiling. Was there anything his roommate *didn't* know about this ship?

Emmett's emoto-glasses flashed a suspicious sky blue. "Just how crazy did it go?"

"Pretty wild from what Sidril told me!" exclaimed Aunt Marisol. "Fanchon and Cruz had to leap from it *while* it was in motion!"

Three jaws fell.

"It's not as scary as it sounds," said Cruz. "Mell was able to slow it down before we jumped. We made it into the main lab no sweat."

"The merry-go-lab has been shut down," said his aunt. "Nobody is allowed back in until they figure out what went wrong with the rotating mechanism."

"Isn't it off-limits to explorers anyway?" Emmett's glasses went a deeper blue.

"It is." Aunt Marisol raised an eyebrow at Cruz.

Everyone was staring at him. "I was ... uh ... helping Fanchon," sputtered Cruz. "All I saw was the storage section. Honest. Totally boring." He pretended to yawn.

Cruz knew he had to be careful what he said around his aunt until he knew for sure she wasn't an agent for Nebula. His only comfort was that he was certain Aunt Marisol would never deliberately hurt him or anyone else. Cruz could see his aunt was genuinely concerned that Fanchon and he might have been injured in the carousel lab.

By now, Nebula must be aware that *Orion*'s tech lab chief knew about Cruz's mom's formula. They'd be worried that Fanchon would try to duplicate the serum. Maybe Aunt Marisol's plan was simply to disable the merry-go-lab so Fanchon couldn't complete her work. She didn't think anyone would get trapped inside. Nebula must have threatened to harm Cruz or his father if she didn't cooperate. Cruz was in danger, and Aunt Marisol was trying to protect him. *If* Aunt Marisol was working for Nebula, it was because she had to. Not because she wanted to. It was the only thing that made sense, the only thing Cruz would allow himself to believe.

"Professor Coronado!" Lani was waving Cruz's aunt over to the desk.

Cringing, Cruz shook his head at his best friend. If Aunt Marisol *was* Zebra, danger or no danger, they were about to tell Nebula where to find the seventh piece of the cipher ...

Too late! Aunt Marisol was already heading over to Lani. Cruz noticed his aunt had on a pair of black-and-white-pinstriped flats with her black knee skirt. Had she worn the daisy sandals today in class? Cruz didn't think so but couldn't be certain.

Aunt Marisol instantly recognized the image on the aqua parchment, as Cruz knew she would. "The Terra-Cotta Army!" she sang. "I traveled to the museum with an excavation team a few years ago. It was incredible. Do you remember what I sent you, Cruz?"

"How could I forget?" He turned to his friends. "Instead of a postcard to decode, she wrote Chinese characters on bamboo the way they did more than two thousand years ago. I had to figure out which script style she was using, then sort through tons of Chinese characters to figure out the message. Aunt Marisol, it was one of your hardest ones ever."

"It was no picnic for me either." His aunt chuckled. "Those lishu characters were tough to master. I had to brush up on my calligraphy skills."

Cruz spun, locking eyes with Lani. *Calligraphy!*

Bending over his mother's box, he quickly found the onyx paintbrush, then went back to the image. The way the warrior held his hand, the space between his thumb and index finger—it had to be! *This* brush belonged *there*! Cruz glanced at Lani. She eagerly nodded to say she thought so, too.

"Is this photo a clue from your mom?" Aunt Marisol's head was beside his.

Cruz could hardly deny it now. "Yes."

"You're sure?"

"Positive," said Sailor. "She even gave us GPS coordinates."

"I see." Aunt Marisol's smile dimmed.

"What's wrong?" asked Emmett.

"Several things. Security, for one." She pointed to the image. "See these dirt walls? The statutes are located in a deep pit. The site has three pits, that we know of. When Shi Huang Di died, the Terra-Cotta Army was buried near his tomb. The statues were placed standing up, as if it were the real imperial army preparing for attack," said his aunt. "And that's how it remained until its discovery in the 1970s. Since then, archaeologists have been carefully excavating the site. Several buildings have been constructed around the pits, and tourists are kept well above the statues on walkways. Only scientists and official personnel are allowed in the pit areas."

"Professor Coronado, couldn't you get us in?" asked Emmett. "I mean, you are an archaeologist with the Academy, and you *have* been there before—"

"That would solve another problem," broke in Sailor. "Dr. Hightower. She hasn't been thrilled about letting us go by ourselves to find the pieces."

Cruz was torn. Emmett and Sailor were right. Aunt Marisol could be a big help to them, but if she *was* working for Nebula, she'd be a far bigger hindrance.

"I could go," Aunt Marisol said wistfully. "We'd need to get permission from Chinese officials and the museum and, yes, of course, there's Dr. Hightower. She's not going to be pleased. There's no way we can get to Xi'an and back to the ship in a weekend."

"We don't have to," clipped Emmett. "Next week is EAC week."

"Eek week?" Lani made the same mistake Cruz had when he'd first heard it.

"That's a hard *c*, Lani," corrected Aunt Marisol. "EAC week as in *E-A-C*. It stands for explorer-adviser conferences. Twice a semester, we close school for a couple of days to give each of you time to meet with your adviser one-on-one. It's basically a check-in, a chance to talk about any issues you want to discuss regarding school, friends, home, whatever. It's also an opportunity for you to catch up on any assignments you missed due to illness or to redo ones your professors weren't happy with. Those couple of days should be enough time for us to make it to China and back. You didn't do EACs at the beginning of the first semester because you were in training at Academy head-quarters, and you couldn't do it at the end of the semester because..." She trailed off.

They all knew why, of course.

"There's another problem," Aunt Marisol went on. "Do you realize how many statues are at the museum?"

Cruz wasn't sure, but he knew it was a lot. "Um ... a few hundred?"

"Try six *thousand*," corrected his aunt.

"Crikey!" gasped Sailor.

"And they're still excavating," said Aunt Marisol. "We think there are a couple thousand more to unearth. The main pit alone, where this warrior is most likely to be, is two football fields long. It's filled with full-size soldiers and officers, like these in your photo, along with hun-dreds of horses and chariots."

"Maybe someone at the museum could help us find this one," said Lani.

"Possibly, but could we trust them?" Aunt Marisol shook her head. "No, if I can get us access to the pits, we'll have to search for the warrior on our own. We'll probably have less than a day, and I doubt that's enough time to find him—"

"Mell could do it," piped up Lani.

"She's fast," agreed Cruz. "And small. No one would notice her. Plus, she wouldn't touch or damage any of the statues on her flight path."

"Sweet as!" Sailor collapsed into one of the navy chairs, flung her feet up onto the little round table, and crossed her ankles. She brushed her hands together. "Our problems are solved."

"Not quite," said Aunt Marisol. She was studying the photo again.

"The stone medallion the warrior is wearing ... I've never seen one like it. Not that it comes as a total surprise. One of the things that makes the clay army so remarkable is that each warrior is unique. They vary in facial features, hairstyle, clothing, and poses. If this red stone is what I think it is ..."

Cruz stared at her. "What is it?"

She glanced up. "Dragon's blood."

"Huh?"

"An ancient term for cinnabar. It's a type of mineral."

Cruz had never heard of cinnabar, but it must be cool. Emmett's emoto-glasses were two large spinning whirlpools of white, blue, and purple.

"Great name." Sailor tugged on her ear lobe. "I need some dragon's blood earrings."

Lani nodded. "It is a beautiful stone."

"It's also a deadly one," said Emmett. "Cinnabar is made of mercury sulfide."

No wonder the emoto-frames were flipping out. Cruz knew what mercury was: the toxic, silvery liquid metal once used in thermometers.

"Centuries ago, alchemists extracted the mercury from cinnabar in their efforts to try to turn metals into gold," explained Aunt Marisol. "It didn't work, of course, but the ancients found plenty of other uses for cinnabar. It was carved into jewelry, crushed into powder to make the red pigment vermilion, and, ironically, was an ingredient in traditional Chinese medicine."

Still seated behind Cruz's desk, Lani glanced up. "Didn't people know how dangerous it was?"

"They did," replied Aunt Marisol. "Although it's unlikely they were as fully aware of its toxicity as we are today. People desperate to cure a disease will try just about anything. Emperor Shi Huang Di *was* desperate, but not because he was ill. His quest was far different. He was searching for the secret to immortality."

Goose bumps fluttered down Cruz's arms.

"The emperor was obsessed with finding a way to live forever," continued his aunt. "Ancient texts say he often drank potions laced with dragon's blood given to him by his alchemists. Unfortunately, the very thing he hoped would prolong his life most certainly cut it short. The emperor died at the age of forty-nine, likely of mercury poisoning." She lifted a shoulder. "Of course, we can't know for certain. Old manuscripts say the emperor's tomb is lined with pearls to re-create the stars in the sky and mercury to simulate the rivers and seas. Soil tests have confirmed high mercury levels within the burial mound, which is about a mile from the Terra-Cotta Army. Given the contamination, officials have decided it's best not to open the tomb for now—maybe forever."

Sailor was hanging over the arm of her chair. "Truth really is stranger than fiction."

"Isn't it?" Aunt Marisol's eyes sparkled. "Archaeology is so much more than digging up bones and artifacts. It's about history and legends. Love and hate. Joy and tragedy. Life and death!"

Cruz loved it when his aunt got pumped up about her work. It got him excited, too.

Lani was twisting her silver lock of hair. "If the stone *is* dragon's blood, what do we do?"

"You don't touch it, that's for sure. We know mercury sulfide can be absorbed through the skin, but we don't know what level, if any, is safe. Plus, sometimes the minerals contain small drops of liquid mercury, which can release harmful vapors."

"It's not dragon's blood," said Cruz. "It can't be. Mom wouldn't have hidden a piece of the stone near something poisonous."

"She might have been in a hurry and had no choice," said his aunt. "Or she could have mistaken it for rhodonite or chalcedony. I don't know. I could be wrong. It might not be cinnabar, but we're not taking any chances. We'll take along safety gloves, however I also need you all to promise that you will not let your bare skin come in contact with the medallion."

Cruz groaned. "But, Aunt Marisol—"

"No, Cruz. No negotiating on this one."

He let out an exasperated sigh. What if the seventh piece of the cipher was behind the cinnabar stone? China's first emperor may not have found the secret to eternal life, but Petra Coronado had. Cruz was living proof of that. He might be the one person in the world who *could* safely handle mercury—something his mother must have known. He couldn't say that, though. That was the worst part. He couldn't say anything about his powers. Cruz had no choice but to bite his tongue.

Aunt Marisol was waiting, her lips in a thin, firm line.

"I won't touch it," vowed Lani.

"Me either," echoed Emmett.

"No worries here, mates," said Sailor. "I'll pass on the dragon's blood jewelry, too, thank you very much."

Aunt Marisol's gaze fell on Cruz.

It was always going to be this way, wasn't it? He would never be able to tell anyone what he could do—what he was.

"I promise," surrendered Cruz.

Was that blood he tasted?

10

CRUZ STARED at his empty screen.
Class was almost over, and he hadn't taken a single note on Professor
Ishikawa's lecture on how marine animals camouflage themselves.

He couldn't stop thinking about Aunt Marisol. She wasn't a spy for
Nebula. It was simply not possible. She would never betray him. His aunt
had done everything she could to help him find his mom's formula,
hadn't she? She'd dutifully kept the box of his mother's things for
seven years to give to him as instructed. Still, it was a bit strange that
she'd *never* opened the box. Not even once? If she had, she would have
discovered it contained her missing Aztec crown charm. But it was
Aunt Marisol who'd arranged for Cruz to go to the wildlife conservation
center in Namibia. On the other hand, she'd also forbidden him to go
to Sossusvlei, where his mother's clue clearly led. Now she was going
to accompany Cruz and his friends to Xi'an, but only after trying to
discourage them from going with all that talk about the dragon's blood
stone. Cruz wasn't sure what to think.

Emmett was tapping Cruz's hand with his stylus. "Smell it?"

Cruz sniffed the air. Chef Kristos's famous five-cheese macaroni.
Ordinarily, he'd be racing Emmett to the dining room the second their
professor dismissed them to lunch, but today Cruz wasn't hungry.

Apparently, neither was Bryndis. "I'll catch up with you guys later,"
she said, turning right out of the classroom instead of left with the

rest of the team. She began walking backward down the hall. "I…uh… have something I have to do."

"Where's she going?" Emmett asked Cruz, who shrugged and looked at Sailor.

She raised her right hand. "Sworn to secrecy."

"Not even a hint?" pressed Lani.

"I shouldn't… Okay, it has to do with a holiday. I'm not saying another word."

A holiday? Today was the 13th of February. She wouldn't be talking about…

"As in, one that's coming up," said Sailor, "you know, with hearts and flowers…"

"She means Valentine's Day." Dugan slapped Cruz between the shoulder blades.

"I figured," said Cruz. "Are you sure, Sailor? They don't have Valentine's Day in Iceland."

Lani handed him a tray. "They don't?"

"They celebrate Konudagur," said Cruz. "It means 'Women's Day.' It's basically the same thing as Valentine's Day, but it's not for another two weeks."

"Konudagur may be in two weeks," said Sailor, "but since Valentine's Day is tomorrow and you're American, she wanted to do something for you."

"Like?" prodded Dugan.

"I really shouldn't spoil it…" Sailor sighed. "Okay, she's making Cruz a valentine card and that's all I'm saying."

"Awww," gushed Lani. "That's sweet."

Cruz reached for a plate of steaming macaroni. "What should I—"

"*Buy* her one in return," said Emmett. "I've seen how you draw."

"You could get her candy, too," offered Sailor. "She likes jelly beans."

The ship's store had them. Cruz remembered that the first time he'd met Fanchon she was eating pink jelly beans she'd bought at *Orion's* little store on the fourth deck of the ship.

"Get her the ones that taste like dirt," teased Dugan.

Emmett chuckled. "Either those or liver and onions."

"I gotta go with burnt toast," said Cruz.

"Burnt *anything*," snickered Lani.

"Snot's the worst!" groaned Sailor.

Settling in at their usual table, Cruz saw that across the dining room Aunt Marisol was eating lunch with Professor Luben. He wondered if his conservation teacher would be giving his aunt a valentine. Or vice versa. It seemed weird to think of his aunt in love. Or even like. Wasn't she kind of old for that stuff?

Dugan elbowed Cruz. "Hey, is there a Men's Day in Iceland?"

"Yep," he replied. "Bóndadagur. It was two weeks ago."

Glancing at Sailor, Dugan gave her a sad face. "You didn't get me anything."

"Next year, I'll get you a big bag of snot-flavored jelly beans," she said. "Unless they have the ones that always remind me of you."

"Which are...?"

"Loud burps that smell like cheese nachos."

Dugan laughed so hard he fell sideways out of his chair.

CRUZ HELD HIS WRIST UP to the security scanner and heard the latch to the tech lab door release. Once inside, it took a few minutes for his eyes to adjust to the eerie green glow. Fanchon had asked him to come by the tech lab before bedtime.

Moments prior to heading up to the fourth deck, Cruz had received a secure message from Dr. Hightower. Aunt Marisol, Cruz, Emmett, Sailor, and Lani had received it, too. Their trip to Xi'an was all set. The president of the Academy had been able to get permission for one of the museum's archaeologists to escort them into the Terra-Cotta Army pits. Their new adviser had been told that the Society's museum in Washington, D.C., was requesting some photos to accompany an upcoming exhibit that featured several of the warriors (which was true). The student photographers—Cruz, Emmett, Lani, and Sailor—would all be receiving class credit and would make up their EAC sessions with Nyomie upon their return. They would leave early Saturday morning and return Wednesday night, with a certain cipher, if all went as Cruz hoped.

In the green haze, Cruz saw Dr. Vanderwick striding toward him. She wore a white lab coat over a blue button-down shirt and black skirt. Clear covers protected a pair of black denim shoes with red roses.

"Hi … Cruz." Dr. Vanderwick was out of breath. "Fanchon will be out in a minute. She's finishing up another experiment. We've been working with the sensotivia gel."

"How's it going?"

"We have a ways to go."

Cruz had a question he'd been longing to ask since he'd first met—was that the right word for it?—the orange goo. "What exactly are you going to do with the gel?"

"We're developing a calming embrocation to initiate a positive neurological response opposing a person's inclination toward negative emotional perceptions."

He gave her a puzzled frown.

"A cream to improve your mood," she quickly translated. "Say you're feeling a bit sad, you rub a little of it into your skin and it'll help cheer you up. If you're scared, it'll give you a boost of confidence. If you're worried, it will soothe you, and so on."

"Cool!"

"It will be if we can figure out how to get it to react in opposition to a person's feelings." She shook her head. "Right now, it's echoing and amplifying negative emotions. We're thinking of calling it emotion lotion, *if* we can work out the kinks."

"Great name," said Cruz. "I hope you get it to work."

She gave him a half grin. "We will. Just a matter of time. And patience."

Dr. Vanderwick may not have been as flashy or fun as Fanchon, but she was almost as brilliant. Cruz knew she was equally responsible for developing much of the gear the explorers used, from their mind-control cameras to hide-and-seek jackets to time capsules. She was also continuing to work on the Universal Cetacean Communicator. Even though he'd nearly drowned after Nebula had sabotaged their proto-type, Cruz was eager to try again whenever the pair had a new version of the helmet ready. He was about to ask her how things were progress-ing with the UCC when he spotted Fanchon coming his way.

Pulling off a pair of purple gloves, she pushed her purple safety goggles up over a head scarf covered in a pastel print of conversation hearts. The front of her light pink apron had three rows of red squares labeled with elements from the periodic table:

LA (lanthanum) + B (boron)

I (iodine) + S (sulfur)

F (fluorine) + U (uranium) + N (nitrogen)

Cruz got it. *LAB IS FUN!*

"Why don't you go on home?" Fanchon urged her assistant. "I'll take care of things here and lock up."

"Thanks. There's a hot bubble bath with my name on it," Dr. Vanderwick snagged her tablet and coffee cup. "See you in the morning."

Once they were alone, Cruz asked about the merry-go-lab. "Is it fixed?"

"Uh ... not yet," said Fanchon. "We had to move everything out of it, which is why this place is in a bit of disarray."

"Do you know what happened?"

"Maintenance says something blew on the braking system." She rolled her eyes. "Obviously. It's a major repair job. But don't worry. We're putting an emergency brake in each room and new safety protocols into place to make sure it's safe."

He stuffed his hands in his pockets. "So you're ... uh ... sure it was an accident?"

"As far as I know."

Maybe Aunt Marisol didn't have anything to do with the merry-go-lab going berserk after all!

Fanchon was studying him. "Cruz, do you know something about what happened?"

"No!" he shot. "I wish I did."

She nodded yet still eyed him with uncertainty. "I asked you to come by tonight because I need a favor."

"Shoot."

"I thought you might be willing to test out a new invention for me." Fanchon reached into the wide front pocket of her pink apron and brought out a black hinged box. She opened the box. Resting on a small black velvet pillow was a brass compass no bigger than a slice of pepperoni. It may have been small, but it was beautiful. Several intertwining strands of brass ivy curled around the circumference of the instrument. They met at the top beneath the nest of a sleeping dove, her head tucked into her wing. The magnetic double-pointed needle, half red and half black, hovered above a white face inlaid with an eight-pointed star. The star appeared to be made from opal, turquoise, and onyx gemstones. Gold script letters labeled each point on the star: *N, NE, E, SE, S, SW, W, NW.*

"I know you usually use your GPS pin for directions," said Fanchon, "but this is not an ordinary compass. See the bird on top. Press it in and hold it for three seconds and the compass becomes a virtugraph."

"Virtugraph?"

"My own terminology. Think of it as a mini polygraph."

"Like one of those machines they hook you up to to find out if you're lying?"

"That's right. Lying triggers certain biological and behavioral changes. When you lie, your pulse and blood pressure increase, you start to sweat, you breathe faster, blink less, and fidget more," explained Fanchon. "The virtugraph registers about a dozen of these 'tells' and interprets them within seconds. If someone is being honest, the red needle will point toward that person, the way the red arrow in a real compass points to true north. If they're lying, they'll get the opposite point, the black needle."

"A truth compass!" exclaimed Cruz. "What a great idea!"

"We'll see," said Fanchon. "I thought you could give this prototype a try for a few months and report back how it works. If you want to, that is."

If he wanted to? Was she kidding?

"Absolutely!" cried Cruz.

"Now, I ... uh ... don't want the other explorers to think I'm showing favoritism, so if you could not mention what it really is or who let you test it—"

"I won't even tell Emmett." Cruz lifted the wisp of a circle from its velvet bed. "It's so light."

"Like the tardigrade, it's sturdier than it looks. It won't break, crack, or dent. It's waterproof and weatherproof, too. Unlike the tardigrade, however, I wouldn't take it into outer space."

Cradling it in his left palm, it took only the tiniest flick of his finger for Cruz to turn the brass compass over. He saw that the smooth back plate was engraved: *Seek truth and you will never lose your way.*

Cruz slid the virtugraph in the right front pocket of his pants and headed for the door. "Thanks again, Fanchon. I'll keep notes on how the virtugraph does."

"I'd appreciate that. And, Cruz?"

"Don't go looking for trouble. The compass may be indestructible, but you're not." She lifted an eyebrow. "Are you?"

"Uh … it's almost curfew. See ya, Fanchon!" Cruz took off.

He was opening the door to his cabin when he realized he'd been so distracted by the virtugraph that he'd forgotten the other reason he'd gone up to the fourth deck: Bryndis's valentine. He was about to go back up to the ship's store on the fourth deck when a flash of red on the floor caught his eye. An envelope. Cruz bent to see his name written on the front. Ah! His card from Bryndis.

Cruz looked toward the open bathroom. "Emmett?"

No answer. He checked the veranda. He was alone. Cruz shut the door and went to sit on his bed to open the sealed envelope. On the front of the card, two frogs were perched on a lily pad, hugging. Inside, the printed message read: *You're TOAD-ally awesome. Hoppy Valentine's Day!*

Cruz smiled, his eyes moving to the handwritten note in red ink at the bottom of the card:

Nebula knows where to find the seventh piece.
They're trying to get there ahead of you. And get rid of you if they can.
I'll do my best to slow them down. Don't die on me now, CC.

—R

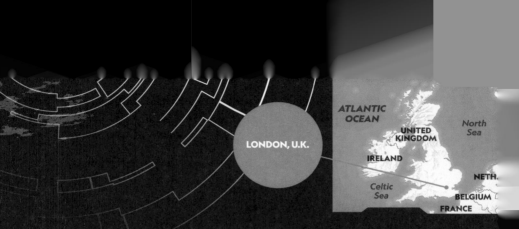

ATLANTIC
OCEAN

North
Sea

UNITED
KINGDOM

LONDON, U.K.

IRELAND

NETH.

Celtic
Sea

BELGIUM

FRANCE

▶THORNE PRESCOTT'S

blue eyes tracked the white jet speeding down the runway. He watched the aircraft leave the ground and soar effortlessly upward. Within seconds, the fuselage vanished into the gray clouds smothering London. Prescott wished he were on that plane. He had no idea where it was going. That's why he wished he were on it.

Reluctantly, he turned to face a glass-roofed building full of strangers. Some were eating. Some dozing. Most had their heads bent over their screens. Feeling his phone buzz in his hand, Prescott answered with a simple "Yes?"

"I may have blown my cover."

"Hold on." Prescott slung his bag over his shoulder and moved down the row to several empty chairs. He tossed his bag onto the end seat. "What happened?"

"Let's just say what goes around comes around." He heard a nervous laugh. "I'm raising suspicions. If I don't step into the shadows now, someone is bound to discover who I am and what I'm up to."

"Does Lion know?" Prescott kept his voice controlled, though he was feeling anything but calm. If Zebra dropped from sight, he would lose his only contact on board Orion.

"You know he's gone dark."

Hezekiah Brume, code name Lion, had left specific instructions not to contact him directly. The head of Nebula said it was business. He said it had nothing to do with Cruz Coronado. Prescott wasn't buying it. He also didn't believe that Zebra wouldn't touch

A blond girl wearing a faded olive army jacket, jeans, and bright pink sneakers was coming down the aisle. One hand held her phone. The other wheeled a white suitcase printed with confetti behind her. The teen dropped into a chair three seats from his, never looking up from her phone. She stretched out her legs, resting her heels on the windowsill. Prescott casually strolled to the corner a few feet away.

"Rendezvous at the original coordinates with Komodo and Scorpion," continued Zebra. "Get the stone. I'll do what I can to slow things down, but it'll have to be more subtle than we'd planned. I can't take any more risks."

"I'll do my job," he bit.

"You'd better, because if Cruz finds this piece, he's only got one more to go."

"I can count," Prescott said coolly. "What about our friendly?"

"Jaguar is fine, for the moment."

"How do I reach—"

"You don't. You know Lion's directive: Protect Jaguar, at all costs. You're on your own, Cobra. Zàijiàn."

He heard a blip. Zebra was gone.

Prescott didn't like this. Zebra was Prescott's only connection to Jaguar, who was feeding them critical information about Cruz's plans. Without Jaguar's intel, Prescott really was on his own. He had to find a way to get in touch with the young agent directly. But how?

All of this was giving Prescott a headache. Or it could have been caffeine withdrawal. He turned back to his chair. Reaching for his bag, he locked eyes with the girl in the army jacket. Her fingers never stopped tapping as she surveyed him for the briefest of moments before returning to her screen. Prescott made his way across the concourse to a small café. He ordered a cup of black coffee. He barely felt the piping hot liquid scald his tongue.

Zebra could be lying. The agent might be getting cold feet or plotting a permanent exit. Or maybe Jaguar had had a change of heart. The explorer might have even threatened to expose them all. That was the problem with the spy game. You never knew what was true. Knowing whom to trust was much simpler: nobody.

Prescott unzipped his bag. His passport was gone. So was the girl.

12

"**WHAT'S** the matter?" asked Lani the second she met Cruz in the explorers' passage.

Cruz shook his head. He never could fool her. Hearing laughter coming from an open cabin behind him, he said, "Not here. Want to come with me up to the ship's store?"

She grinned. "Jelly beans, huh?"

"Yeah, yeah." Cruz punched the button for the elevator.

Once the elevator doors shut with them inside, Cruz hit the button to stop the car. He took Roewyn's card from his pocket and handed it to his best friend.

"It's frustrating," he said, watching her read it. "Nebula always seems to know what I do *before* I do it. I'll bet they know I'm here with you right now."

"Probably," said Lani matter-of-factly. "You can thank Zebra and Jaguar for that."

Zebra. Had Aunt Marisol been the one to tell Nebula where he was going? Cruz hoped not, but how else could they know? He couldn't keep denying it. Cruz had to seriously consider the possibility that his aunt might have done more than sabotage the merry-go-lab. Maybe not all spies were mean, greedy, or deadly. Maybe some worked quietly, planting seeds of doubt or putting small obstacles in your way. One step forward. Two steps back. Maybe some spies were friendly. Or even family.

But what would make her turn against her own nephew? *Why* would she do it?

Lani handed the card back to him. "Do you trust Roewyn?"

"She's been right about everything so far. Plus, if it weren't for her, I'd be a pancake in Petra." Cruz raked a hand through his hair. "You think I shouldn't trust her?"

"She *is* the daughter of the guy who's responsible for your mom's death and who's now trying to destroy you, too. That would make *me* a little nervous."

"You know Roewyn doesn't like what he's doing," said Cruz. "That's why she's helping us."

"I know. She might be telling the truth, but have you thought this through?"

"What do you mean?"

"You're trying to complete the cipher. Roewyn's dad is trying to stop you. Right now, she can secretly help you without her father knowing, but eventually he *will* find out what she's up to. At some point, Roewyn is going to have to decide between her dad and you." Her eyes searched his. "And when that happens, who do you think she's going to choose?"

Cruz shifted.

"Hey." The male voice coming through the elevator's intercom made them jump. "Maintenance here. Is there a problem?"

They looked up at the tiny camera in the corner. Lani tapped the intercom button. "No. We're fine, thanks."

Cruz smacked the red button harder than he needed to. With a jolt, the elevator resumed its upward trek. It stopped at the third deck. When it opened, Nyomie stepped on and hit 5. "Where you guys headed?"

"Deck four," said Cruz.

"Getting a valentine for your valentine, huh?" Nyomie saw Cruz's eyebrows shoot up. "What can I say? It's a small ship."

It seemed to take ages for the door to finally open.

"Bye, guys," said Nyomie.

"Bye," they said. Lani stepped off first.

"Word to the wise?"

Cruz's head snapped around so fast, the nerves in the back of his neck tingled. He was suddenly breathless, as if he'd run all 11 miles up the steep and muddy Kalalau Trail back home. He gawked at Nyomie, the elevator door smacking him in the shoulder. "What ... did ... you say?"

"I said do you mind if I offer you a little advice?"

"Oh!" Cruz could breathe again. "Uh, sure ... I mean no, I don't mind ..."

"You don't have to get Bryndis anything fancy or expensive. Give her something from your heart. Something that could only come from you. It can be small and simple." Her lips turned up at the corners. "In fact, the best things usually are."

Cruz gave her a grateful nod, and the door closed between them with Nyomie still smiling.

"ARE WE THERE YET?" Sailor let her duffel and backpack fall onto the white-and-gold speckled tiles before melting into a chair.

"Almost," said Cruz, scanning the airport lobby for a pair of snake-skin-print cowboy boots or anyone suspicious. He was tired, too, but he knew how dangerous it was to let down his guard. Sailor's head was swiveling almost as fast as Cruz's. His friends now knew about Roewyn's warning.

It had been a long travel day. Aunt Marisol, Cruz, Emmett, Sailor, and Lani had met at the ship's helicopter pad at five that morning so Captain Roxas could fly them to Jakarta, Indonesia. From there, they got on *Condor*, the Academy's jet. *Condor* was already scheduled to transport *Endeavor*'s senior explorers on a mission, so it could only take the group as far as Bangkok, Thailand. They'd spent nearly five hours in the Suvarnabhumi Airport, which Emmett declared was like being in the stomach of a glass caterpillar, before boarding a commercial flight to Xi'an Xianyang International Airport. Finally, they had arrived! All that was left was to get everyone through customs, grab an Auto Auto to the hotel, have a quick bite, and crash. Tomorrow afternoon, they'd head to the Terra-Cotta Army museum to meet Dr. Hightower's archaeologist friend, who would be able to get them into the pits.

Here came Lani. She'd spotted Sailor and Cruz and was trudging toward them, her hide-and-seek jacket slung over one shoulder and the straps of her backpack and duffel over the other. Like them, her gaze was sweeping the room.

"There's Emmett," said Sailor.

About 20 feet behind Lani, Emmett was just coming out of the customs area. Seeing them, he broke into a jog. He caught up with Lani and said something to her, and they both hurried the rest of the way. Cruz could tell something was wrong. The emoto-glasses looked like a brewing storm of thick gray cumulonimbus clouds.

"Your ... aunt ... she ..." huffed Emmett. "They're detaining her ... I don't know why ..."

Cruz reached for his stuff. "Come on, let's go back."

"You can't ... They won't let you back in ..." gasped Emmett. "Besides, she said not to ... She told me to tell you to go to the hotel ... It's safer. She'll meet us there."

"She must suspect Nebula is behind this," said Lani.

"What *exactly* happened?" pressed Cruz.

"I'm not totally sure," said Emmett. "My Mandarin is a little rusty. I'd put my jacket in my bag to go through screening, so I didn't have my translator on me. I think there was a problem with her passport. The officials didn't seem mad or anything. They weren't handcuffing her. Maybe it expired?"

"She wouldn't have been able to travel with Explorer Academy without a current passport," said Sailor. "But they might have mistaken her for someone else. That happened to my cousin once—same name, age, and everything."

Cruz furrowed his brow. "How many Marisol Coronados could there be in the world?"

Lani shrugged. "There only needs to be two."

"I'm sure Professor Coronado will straighten everything out." Emmett was scanning the area. "I think we should do as she says and go on to the hotel."

Cruz shook his head. He didn't want to leave without his aunt.

"Do you really want to hang around an airport knowing that Nebula could show up at any minute?" Sailor whispered between gritted teeth. "We should go."

Cruz was hungry and tired. He couldn't think straight. It did seem to make sense to leave before Nebula spotted them, but Aunt Marisol...

"It'll be okay." Lani put a hand on Cruz's arm. "We can call Dr. Hightower from the hotel. Let's get out of here."

"I guess," he surrendered.

They found the Auto Auto kiosk outside the east terminal entrance. The frosty night air sent a chill through Cruz. Their car resembled a snow cone tipped on its side, in both style and size. There was barely enough room for the four of them to cram inside the "snow" part of the cone. Lani and Sailor hopped in the front, while Cruz squished into the back seat with Emmett. He had to hold his backpack on his lap.

"*Huānyíng,*" said the male voice of the onboard computer.

"English, please," requested Sailor, her tablet in hand. "Take us to Mèngxiǎng Hotel."

"It is forty-point-three kilometers, or twenty-five miles, to Mèngxiǎng Hotel," said the computer. "It will require approximately forty-nine minutes to reach your destination. Please note that you have arrived on the final day of the Spring Festival, or Lunar New Year. Due to the influx of tourists, traffic into and around the city may be rerouted or heavier than normal. Thank you for choosing Auto Auto and enjoy your ride."

Cruz unzipped the side of his pack and found his tablet. There were no messages from his aunt. He tried calling her. She didn't answer. Cruz then dialed Dr. Hightower's private cell phone number. Again, no answer.

"Academy headquarters is thirteen hours behind us," said Emmett.

The boys exchanged concerned looks. If it was nine in the morning in Washington, D.C., Dr. Hightower should have picked up. Where could she be?

"Should I call my dad?" asked Cruz.

"You'll only worry him," replied Emmett. "And wake him. Let's wait until we get to the hotel. If we haven't heard anything from your aunt by then..."

Traffic *was* heavy, but the view along the route was beautiful. It seemed every building, from the smallest café to the tallest skyscraper, was lit for the festival. The bare trees lining the streets dripped with thousands of white diamond lights. Colorful globe lanterns swung from branches and lampposts. They drove past a park where an enormous glowing red-and-yellow dragon rose from a lake like a serpent from the deep, its reflection rippling across the dark waters. Dozens of search beams fanned across the clear night sky, creating a checkerboard of lights. Every now and then they heard the crackle of fireworks and

looked up to see blue, gold, red, and green starbursts. As they got closer to the city, the sidewalks became more crowded. Most of the people were tourists, dressed in winter clothes, but many wore elaborate, brightly colored costumes. Feathers sprouted from oversize masks of lions, dragons, birds, and other animals. A group of young children with filmy purple butterfly wings on their backs skipped alongside their slow-moving car. The kids waved. Cruz lifted a hand in return. At one intersection, several teen girls in red silk robes embroidered with pink lotus flowers crossed in front of them. Any other time, Cruz would have absorbed everything, but tonight the vivid colors, blurred lights, and continuous movement overwhelmed his senses. He shut his eyes.

"You have arrived at your destination," said the dashboard computer. "The current air temperature in Xi'an is thirty-six degrees Fahrenheit, and the time is ten thirty-two p.m. This vehicle will remain for your use for the next four days. Thank you for choosing Auto Auto."

Cruz reached for the door handle.

"Stop!" cried Lani. "Nobody get out of the car."

Cruz leaned forward. "Lani, what's the matt—"

"Nebula. They're here."

13

XI'AN, CHINA

RUSSIA
KAZAKHSTAN
MONGOLIA
JAPAN
PAKISTAN
CHINA
TAIWAN
INDIA
Philippine Sea
MYANMAR
(BURMA)
South
China
Sea

"WHERE?" Cruz, Emmett, and Sailor were

spinning in their seats. "Where?"

"Auto Auto, lock the doors," ordered Lani, her eyes swiftly moving from the rearview mirror to her side-view mirror and back again. They heard the latches go down. "Computer, find us another hotel. Anything ... anywhere around here ... and hurry."

"One moment, please, while I search for—"

"There's no time," barked Lani. "Where is the busiest place in Xi'an?"

"The most populous location, at present, is the lantern fair at the Xi'an City Wall."

"Go there. *Now!*"

"Destination confirmed." The car signaled and eased smoothly out into traffic. "It is eight kilometers, or five miles, to the Yongning entrance of the Xi'an City Wall. Due to heavier-than-normal traffic, it will require approximately twenty-two minutes to reach—"

"Fine, fine, just go!"

Once they were underway, Lani half turned in her seat. "A man was crossing the street across from the hotel when we pulled up. I recognized him. He was one of your dad's kidnappers, Cruz—the one I saw being arrested at the Gemini Observatory."

Nobody had to ask if she was sure. Her tone left little doubt.

"I figured while we're waiting for Auto Auto to find a new hotel for us, the next best thing was a public place with a big crowd," said Lani. "Maybe we can lose them at the festival."

Turning to look out the back window, Cruz was blinded by headlights. Were they being followed? Probably. In this gridlock, it wouldn't take Nebula long to catch up to them.

Cruz tried calling his aunt again. She did not pick up. He tried Dr. Hightower again, too. Still no luck. Cruz sent the Academy president a short message, explaining that Aunt Marisol was stuck in customs and could use her help. He did not mention that they were on the run from Nebula. One crisis at a time.

"Thank you for your patience," said the dashboard computer. "Because of the high volume of tourists in town for the Spring Festival, there are no available rooms in any hotel, lodge, or bed-and-breakfast within a ten-mile radius of Xi'an. Would you like to expand your search area?"

"Yes," said Lani. "Keep looking."

"Crikey!" Sailor's face was practically glued to the windshield.

They were heading straight for a massive stone wall! Cruz figured it had to be 40 or 50 feet high. Several pagoda watchtowers were spaced out along the wall's U-shaped arches. Between the towers stretched a row of giant illuminated figures—pandas, dragons, birds, horses, lotus flowers, Chinese symbols. These were the lanterns? They rose 10, 20, even 30 feet into the darkness! It was like a big, glowing parade, except the lanterns weren't moving. As the car passed beneath one of the wall's high archways, Cruz tapped his GPS pin. The badge emitted a holo-beam onto his window:

The Xi'an City Wall, also known as the Fortifications of Xi'an, is one of the largest military defensive walls in the world and the most complete ancient city wall still standing in China. It was built mostly in the 14th century to protect Xi'an, the capital of Shaanxi Province and home to 13 dynasties. The square-shaped fortification is nearly 40 feet tall, 46 feet wide, and contains 5.4 square miles of the city. It features watchtowers, battlements, and a 60-foot-wide moat, complete with drawbridges.

Tourists visit the wall to enjoy the view, take photos, and bike around the top (it takes about two hours to complete the bike route).

Their snow-cone car was stopping along the curb next to the largest pagoda. The open area was teeming with pedestrians and bicyclists. "You have arrived at your destination," announced the dashboard computer, unlocking the doors. "The time is ten fifty-six p.m. and the outside

temperature is thirty-five degrees Fahrenheit. We are still looking for an available hotel and will alert you when one has been located. This vehicle will now park. For pickup, please use the access code sent to your phone. Thank you for choosing Auto Auto."

"I see the steps going up to the top of the wall." Emmett pushed open his door.

"Stop!" Lani shouted again.

Sailor let out groan. "Don't tell me Nebula's here, too!"

"I haven't seen anyone, but it wouldn't surprise me," said Lani. "No, I was thinking about something else. Cruz said Nebula always seems to know what he does before he does it. It's true. They had to have known where and when we were arriving tonight to stop Professor Coronado. And obviously they know what hotel we booked..."

"Obviously," sighed Cruz.

"I'll bet they know when we're due at the Terra-Cotta Army museum," said Lani. "It seems to me the only way we're ever going to outwit Nebula is to—"

"Do the opposite of what they expect," said Emmett. He shut his door.

Lani was twirling her silver lock of hair. "If Nebula thinks we're going to be at the Terra-Cotta Army museum tomorrow afternoon, then we need to—"

"Go tonight," decided Cruz.

"Tonight?" Sailor's head appeared around the side of the seat. "But it's closed."

"We'll get in," vowed Emmett, his emoto-glasses shooting off their own yellow, green, and purple fireworks. He reached into the backpack on his lap for his tablet. "Lani?"

She was pulling out her computer, too. "Send me the schematics."

Sailor directed the Auto Auto to take them to the museum.

"The museum is currently closed," said the computer. "It will reopen tomorrow at—"

"We know," she said. "Take us there anyway."

The computer confirmed the destination was 27 miles from their present location and calculated they would arrive in 52 minutes. The car signaled left, and they crawled into traffic once again. There was nothing to do now but wait. Leaning back, Cruz exhaled. They were taking a huge risk going on their own.

If Emmett and Lani couldn't disable the museum's security system...

If Nebula found out what they were up to...

If Aunt Marisol needed their help...

Cruz's tablet was ringing. When he saw who was calling, he fumbled the device, nearly losing it in the crack between his seat and the door. "Aunt Marisol? What happened? Where are you? Are you all right?"

"I'm okay, everything's okay," she soothed. "I'm not in jail. Still stuck at the airport." Cruz put her on speaker. "The good news is that it's a case of mistaken identity."

Sailor popped around the seat to give him a big nod.

"The bad news is it probably won't get straightened out until morning," continued Aunt Marisol. "I have a bed for the night—well, a comfortable lounge chair anyway. I'll get to the hotel as soon as I can. Fortunately, we don't have to be at the museum tomorrow until a few minutes before they close."

"Uh...yeah...r-right," stammered Cruz.

"How about you guys?" asked his aunt. "Everyone all right? You found the hotel okay?"

"We're fine. It's you we're worried about."

"No need. I'm warm and dry. We'll get it sorted out, hon. Get some rest. Love you."

"Good night, *Tía*. Love you, too."

The snow-cone car was slowing. It signaled, then turned into a giant parking lot. In the distance, Cruz could make out the silhouettes of several square, warehouse-like buildings. One had a curved roof, like an airplane hangar. He'd uploaded a map of the museum to his computer and recognized the building as the one that housed pit one. They'd done it! They had made it to the Terra-Cotta Army.

Now the hard part: getting inside.

Sailor was on her tablet. "I'm not picking up any biosignatures out-side. We're alone out here, so far. There are two guards in the security hub and three people in the building that houses pit two. Probably archaeologists working late."

On a Saturday during the Spring Festival? Cruz wasn't so sure.

Emmett was also hunched over his computer, fingers flying.

"How's it going?" asked Cruz.

His roommate did not glance up. "Working on it."

"We'll get it," said Lani. "It might take a little while."

Cruz glanced around the empty parking lot. "Mind if I stretch out?"

"Nope," said Emmett and Lani at the same time.

"I'm coming, too," said Sailor.

"I'll mask your biosignatures," said Lani. "In case they have a security web."

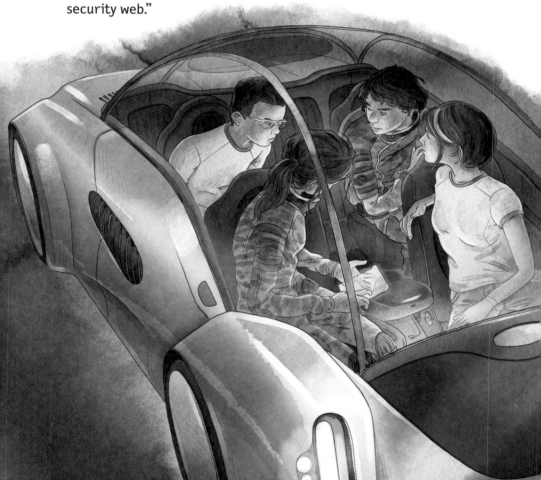

"Don't hesitate to use your shadow badges if you hear or see anything," reminded Emmett.

The second Cruz and Sailor stepped out of the car, they were blasted by a frigid wind. They scrambled to the trunk for their hide-and-seek jackets. Cruz tossed Sailor hers, and the pair turned their thick, reversible coats to the "hide" side: gray camouflage. Cruz tucked his tablet into the big outside pocket, zipped the coat to his neck, and flipped up the hood. He stuck his hands into the front slanted pockets. The coats would keep their bodies toasty warm, but exposed parts, like noses, fingers, and toes wouldn't be protected. Once Sailor was bundled up, too, they ambled across the mega parking lot. The dimly let plain of concrete was a drastic contrast to the fast pace of the city. It was so quiet here. So dark.

Sailor's hood turned Cruz's way. "We don't have the gloves." She was right. He'd forgotten about the protective gloves Fanchon had provided in case they needed to touch the dragon's blood medallion. Aunt Marisol had them in her bag. "What if we have to—"

"I'll do it," said Cruz. "I'll wrap my hands in my shirt or something."

"Your shirt? Will that be enough to protect you?"

"I'll be fine."

"It's just that we promised your aunt—"

"I said I'd be fine."

"Okay," she said meekly.

"Sorry. Guess I'm hungrier than I thought." Cruz started digging in his pockets for a package of trail mix or some mints. Even a stick of gum would be welcome at this point. Sailor glanced up at the three rooflines towering above the courtyard. "I bet they have super-tight security here. Do you think Emmett and Lani will be able to get us in?"

"Hmmm?" Cruz had found something in his pocket. Lifting out his hand, he uncurled his fingers.

Sailor grinned. "Your time capsule."

Cruz shook his head. "Not mine." He must have grabbed Emmett's jacket from the trunk. "I gave mine to Bryndis."

"I know. It's all she's talked about all week."

Shrinking back into his hood, Cruz smiled to himself. He'd taken Nyomie's advice on gift-giving, brainstorming for something small and simple, something from the heart. Cruz thought about all the things that mattered to him: his dad, his aunt, his mom, the holo-dome, his friends, Hubbard, Explorer Academy, the Goofy Foot...

And then it hit him. Surfing!

It was his favorite sport. Even better, Bryndis loved to surf as much as he did. What if he made a card of Hanalei Bay? He could use their 3D printer to create a pop-up card that included the beach, the waves, the pier, and the Goofy Foot. Better still, why not put the memory of his best surfing run onto his time capsule so she could experience the run for herself? And that is exactly what Cruz did.

On Valentine's Day morning, Cruz had stopped by her cabin on his way to breakfast to give her the card and time capsule. He'd expected Bryndis to put the memory keeper away to view later, but she'd watched it right then and there. Closing her eyes and her hand, Bryndis had found herself transported to the teal surf and white-tipped waves of Hanalei, reliving the wildest run of Cruz's life—one where he didn't wipe out but teetered perfectly on the crest of a massive wave as it curled inland. She'd flung out her arms, as if balancing on her own board, nearly smacking Cruz in the face. Once the run had finished, Bryndis had opened her eyes. "I have *got* to surf that bay for real!"

"How about this summer?" Cruz had blurted without thinking.

She'd laughed. "It's a date."

Bryndis had given him a valentine card, as Sailor had said she would, but she'd also given him a gift, too: an oil painting of Hubbard! It was a perfect likeness of the Westie, from his wet button nose to the tip of his perpetually-in-motion tail. Bryndis had painted it on a small five-inch-by-five-inch canvas.

"I hope you like it," she'd said when he'd unwrapped it.

"I love it," Cruz had said.

The painting now sat on Cruz's nightstand, perched on a little wooden easel, next to his silver holo-dome.

Cruz tucked Emmett's time capsule back into his pocket. They'd reached the sprawling brick courtyard that led to the museum's three buildings. The hangar containing pit one was to their far left. As they passed under a lamppost, the little puffs of air they exhaled glowed in the cone of light. Sailor checked her tablet. "We'd better turn back. Nobody's nearby, but they have a security web surrounding each building, and until we know Emmett and Lani have breached it, we don't want to get too close. They could pick up our biosigs."

They headed back to the car.

"You know, Emmett gave me a handmade valentine," said Sailor.

"He did?" Interesting. Emmett hadn't said anything to Cruz about it.

"It has a periodic table on the front," she continued. "Inside it says, 'You must be made of copper and tellurium because you're cute.'"

Cruz got it. "Cu" was the abbreviation for copper and "Te" stood for tellurium. He bet he knew where his roommate had gotten the idea: Fanchon's LAB IS FUN apron.

"I looked up the properties of tellurium," Sailor said, her voice flat. "It's brittle, slightly toxic, and, in gaseous form, smells like garlic."

Cruz laughed. "Hey, don't forget the copper part. Copper's malleable and ductile. If you think about it, you are kind of like that. You bend under stress, but you don't break and you adapt pretty well to change. Yep. You're copper, all right."

She gave him a skeptical raise of the eyebrow.

"Okay, I might be reaching," admitted Cruz, "but don't you think you might be taking it a little too literally? After all, the card did say you were cute."

"True." Sailor sighed. "So, in periodic table terms you're saying

Emmett was being nitrogen plus iodine plus cerium."

Cruz put the abbreviations together: N+I+Ce. "Exactly. He might even lutetium plus vanadium ... plus—what's a *Y*?"

"Yttrium, and if you even think about saying 'oxygen' and 'uranium,' get ready for a plutonium plus nitrogen plus carbon plus hydrogen."

Cruz couldn't help laughing at her rapid-fire delivery as he put it all together: Pu+N+C+H.

He heard a muffled chime. It was coming from his coat. Cruz pulled out his tablet to answer the video call. "Well?"

"Wooooot!" The cheer pierced his eardrum. "We're in!"

CROUCHED in a nasty sticker bush next to

a side door of the hangar, Cruz wasn't nearly as confident as Emmett about their chances for success. He shoved a thorny branch away from his cheek. "Did you guys ... uh ... notice there's a camera above the door?"

"Yep," said Lani, her tablet balanced on her knee. "Not ... a ... problem. I've tapped into the feed and have been recording video of the courtyard. When we're ready, I'll switch the cam over to the recording, and that's what the guards in the security hub will see. It'll play in a loop so we can take whatever time we need to get in and out."

"Sweet as." Sailor rubbed her hands together. "How do we bypass the lock?"

"We don't," answered Emmett, also bent over his tablet. "They've got a state-of-the-art security system. I was lucky to find one lock in this place that didn't use complex biometrics and this is it. It uses a six-digit numeric key code. My program will interface with the system and run through all the possible combinations until it finds the right pass code to unlock, but"—he glanced up—"there's a catch."

Wasn't there always?

"Once I log in," continued Emmett, "we'll have thirty seconds to find the code."

Sailor made a face. "Or ...?"

"It will alert security, sound an alarm they can hear in Xi'an, and we won't make it to the parking lot," clipped Lani.

"Did you say six digits?" gulped Sailor. "That means there are—"

"One million possible combinations," said Emmett.

"Crikey! That'll take—"

"Ten seconds," he said. "More or less. It'll be tight, but we can do it."

Cruz heard the crunch of leaves. He scanned the courtyard. "Are you sure nobody else is here?"

"Checking." Sailor scrolled through her tablet. "All clear outside. Nothing's changed inside either. Besides the guards, the archaeologists in pit two haven't moved."

Lani nudged Emmett. "You ready?"

He sighed. "As I'll ever be."

"I'm transferring from the live feed to the recording," said Lani. They waited a few tense seconds. "Video is up and running. It's yours from here, Emmett."

Emmett's emoto-glasses morphed into determined blue teardrops. "I'm interfacing with the security system ... now!" He tapped a button on his screen, and a gray circle began to spin. In the corner of his screen, a digital clock was counting down from 30 seconds. No one moved. All eyes were glued to the whirling circle and those red digital numbers.

30 ... 29 ... 28 ...

The program started cycling so quickly, the numbers were a blur. The cold air was making Cruz light-headed. Or he might have been forgetting to breathe. When the countdown hit 20 seconds, Cruz watched the door on the side of the building. It didn't move. In the meantime, the program was still searching for the correct six-digit password. Time was ticking away. Cruz was starting to get nervous. He wasn't the only one. Sailor had chewed down her pinkie nail. Lani was clutching her tablet so tightly Cruz feared she would snap it in two.

16 ... 15 ... 14 ...

"Shouldn't it have found it by now?" whispered Sailor.

"It will," insisted Emmett, but his tablet was quivering in his hand.

10 . . . 9 . . . 8 . . .

"We'd better make a run for it." Lani got to her feet. "It's a long way to the car."

Cruz and Sailor hopped up, too.

"Let's go, Emmett." Cruz grabbed Emmett's arm. "You gave it your best shot."

5 . . . 4 . . . 3 . . .

But his roommate wasn't moving. "Just one more—"

"Emmett, come on!"

1 . . . 0.

The spinning circle froze. So did Cruz, though every cell in his body told him it was the wrong thing to do. He should have been sprinting across the courtyard. Security guards would be surrounding them any second. Cruz braced himself for the blare of an alarm.

The door on the side of the building slid aside. Lani was on the move first, followed by Sailor. "Come on, slowpokes," she shot, sprinting past Cruz.

They flew through the door—Lani, Sailor, Emmett, then Cruz. A second after he cleared the entry, Cruz felt wind on the back of his head as the door swept shut behind him. Cruz spotted a railing about 20 feet directly ahead.

The pit! Everyone rushed to the rail. The glow from Emmett's and Lani's tablets revealed the side view of several dozen terra-cotta soldiers, along with a ladder leaning against the other side of the rail. Packed tightly together in the trench, the clay figures faced the front of the building. With Emmett leading the way, the explorers made their way to the front of the exhibit to get their bearings.

More impressive than any photograph, the infantry of statues stretched as far as Cruz could see. They vanished into the darkness. The long flanks were separated by ridged, earthen walls wide enough for a person to walk across. Or maybe crawl over—they were awfully bumpy. The warriors looked so real. Shoulders back and heads high, many had their fingers curled into fists. Aunt Marisol explained this was because they'd once held wooden lances, crossbows, and other weapons. It was as if the army had been frozen in time, as if the soldiers had been dutifully standing at attention for more than 2,000 years, waiting to be called into battle. It gave Cruz an uneasy feeling.

Cruz took out his tablet and opened the upper-right pocket of his uniform. "Mell, on. Come to eye level, please." Before their trip, Cruz had uploaded the photo of the dragon's blood warrior into the drone's memory, along with a diagram of each pit at the museum. Once the MAV began her search for the soldier, Cruz would be able to monitor her metrics, progress, and location from his tablet. "Mell, find the dragon's blood warrior as quickly as you can," he directed. "Once you do, send back video for confirmation. Mell, go."

Flashing her golden eyes twice, the bee did a barrel roll and was off.

She zipped to the left toward the first flank. Cruz watched the twin beacons of her eyes light the way until the drone dropped below his sight line. He opened up her program on his tablet. With Sailor, Emmett, and Lani clustered around him, Cruz flipped on Mell's camera view. Back and forth the tiny bee went, weaving horizontally through the short rows of statues like yarn on a loom. It was a dizzying collage of clay heads and shoulders and arms.

"She's going fast!" exclaimed Lani.

"At this rate, she'll get through the first flank in a couple of minutes," figured Emmett.

With roughly 10 rows to search, it would take Mell about 20 minutes to find the dragon's blood warrior—*if* he was here. They watched Mell make the turn to come up the second flank. Cruz's eyes went from his screen to the pit back to his screen again, anxious for the tiny drone to appear.

"There!" Sailor pointed to the pair of bobbing lights. The bee was flitting between the line of soldiers below them. Making a sharp turn, she headed into the third flank. Cruz switched his computer view to an overhead diagram of the pit. Mell was now a yellow dot on his screen.

"Guys?" rasped Sailor. "I ... uh ... probably should have been paying more attention but ... the three biosignatures in the other building? They're moving. And they seem to be ... coming this way."

"Now you tell us," Emmett said with a snort.

They heard a door behind them open.

"Hide!" hissed Cruz, frantically waving them back the way they'd come.

They took off running. Cruz, Emmett, Lani, and Sailor hurried along the rail, rounded the corner, and took cover behind a row of recycling bins. His heart pounding in his ears, Cruz dared to peer around the bend. He could see two flashlight beams and two figures. One was a good foot shorter than the other and somewhat wider, too.

"You're sure?" said the short guy.

"They're here," answered the other. "I couldn't lock on to their biosigs but I was able to pick up the drone's frequency."

"Mell!" gasped Lani.

Cruz could have slapped himself. "I forgot to mask her signal!"

"I mean she's stopped." Lani was tapping his tablet. She was right. The yellow dot on Cruz's screen was no longer moving. It had paused in the fifth flank about two-thirds of the way back. Cruz hit Mell's camera view. There it was: the dragon's blood medallion!

"Mell found him," Cruz whispered to his friends. He hit the honeycomb remote on his uniform. "Good job, Mell. Shut off your lights and stay put." Cruz lifted his hand off the pin.

"We've got a location. Now we have to figure out how to get past those two."

"We need to draw them away from the warrior," said Lani.

"You mean, like a decoy?" Sailor gulped. "I like it."

"We could use Mell," breathed Emmett. "You three go for the cipher. I'll stay here and fly her around the front of the exhibit to keep them from spotting you."

Cruz didn't like splitting up, but his team was right. They needed to throw Nebula's goons off their trail. Plus, if Mell got injured, she could be fixed, whereas one of them . . .

Unpinning the honeycomb remote from his jacket, Cruz handed it to Emmett. "Good luck."

"You too."

Cruz, Sailor, and Lani went back the way they'd come, creeping down the side of the exhibit until they spotted the ladder near the side door. One by one, the trio went over the rail and down a few rungs of the ladder, before hopping onto the flat top of the first earthen wall.

The statues were six feet tall, and the walls extended another foot or two above their heads. It wasn't a huge drop to the pit floor. However, the top of the wall was filled with ruts and ridges. Also, their only light came from the lampposts outside shining through the upper side windows. It was slow going to make sure they didn't stub a toe or topple over the side. Cruz led the way. He stayed low, his tablet tucked between his forearm and his stomach. Every now and then, he looked back to make sure Lani and Sailor were doing okay.

Cruz was making the turn between the fourth and fifth flanks when he heard a tiny yelp behind him. Spinning on the balls of his feet, he saw Lani flail her arms. He lurched toward her, flung out his hand, and caught Lani's shoulder. But she was falling the other way. If he used both hands, he'd lose his tablet. Lani's knee hit the edge. She was going over! Cruz was about to let go of his computer when, from behind Lani, two arms appeared. They circled her waist. Sailor!

Now steadied, Lani got her feet back under her. That was close!

Once everyone's pulse had settled, they continued along the wall. Cruz took a peek at his tablet. They were almost there. He caught Lani's eye and pointed down. She nodded and passed the message along to Sailor. Cruz found a reasonably flat spot and, putting his tablet in his jacket pocket, got on his stomach. He eased his legs over the edge of the wall, then climbed down—well, slid down—into the trench. There wasn't much in the way of toeholds or handholds. Mere inches separated the statues from the side of the trench, and as Cruz neared the bottom, something poked him in the hip. Turning, he nearly hit his nose on the arm of a warrior. He looked up into a stern stone face.

"Coming down!" whispered Lani to his right. Cruz helped to guide Lani, then Sailor.

The clay soldiers stood shoulder to shoulder, four across. There was little space between the rows as well. Scooting between the statues, Cruz, Lani, and Sailor kept their arms at their sides to avoid touching anything. Aunt Marisol had told them each figure was valued in the millions but, in truth, was priceless. "There may be thousands of them," she'd cautioned, "but none can be replaced."

Suddenly, a hand came around the side of a statue. It grabbed Cruz's sleeve. He jerked back, smacking his elbow on the rocky wall.

"It's me," hissed Sailor. "He's here."

Rubbing his tingling funny bone, Cruz squeezed in beside Sailor and Lani. His gaze was immediately drawn to the cinnabar medallion on the

warrior's chest. Near the top of the scarlet stone, Cruz saw something he hadn't seen in the photo: a diagonal crack. Was it too tiny to show up in his mom's picture? Or had the break happened after she'd taken the photo? Worse, could there be liquid drops in the fracture—enough to create a dangerous gas?

"Cruz!" Lani brought him out of his thoughts.

He dug out the black calligraphy brush from his pocket and gently placed it in the groove between the thumb and first finger of the warrior's right hand. Cruz wasn't sure what to do next.

In the darkness, the explorers stood as motionless as the clay army.

The warrior's hand—it was beginning to move! At first Cruz thought his eyes were playing tricks on him, but he quickly realized the statue's wrist *was* rotating. It slowly revolved counterclockwise, stopping once its palm faced the ceiling.

Ping!

The trio jumped. The hand had sprung forward a few inches from its sleeve, revealing a hollow wrist. Cruz carefully reached up inside the hidden chamber. His fingers touched cloth. Something was inside the fabric. Cruz brought out the object, wrapped in black satin and tied with twine. It was the right size and weight to be one of his mom's pieces. Cruz's hands shook as he freed the knot and pulled off the twine. Drawing in a breath, he peeled back the edges of the cloth one corner at a time . . .

The seventh cipher!

The warrior's now empty wrist began to move again. They watched it reverse its movements, sliding back into its sleeve and returning to its original position. Cruz removed the calligraphy brush and put it in his pocket.

Huddled together, they marveled at the wedge of black marble in Cruz's hand. It may have only been a small stone, but it was their treasure! Cruz took a photo of it, something he now did after finding each piece of his mother's formula. As soon as they were safely in the car, Cruz would send the picture to his dad. It was a safeguard, in case anything ever happened to the original cipher. Or to Cruz.

"We did it." Lani sighed. "We really did it. With so many obstacles, I wasn't sure we could find the stone this time."

Cruz nodded. He'd had his doubts, too.

"Congratulations!" boomed a man's voice.

The explorers spun into a pair of blinding beams of light.

"Guess who?"

Nobody needed to guess.

Two men stood atop the wall: a thin man in a dark knit cap and wool jacket and a shorter bald guy with a steel-wool beard and arms so huge his biceps bulged through his nylon coat. They were the same men that Emmett and Mell were supposed to keep busy—Nebula's men.

"I hope Emmett's okay," whispered Lani.

Cruz did, too.

"Quiet!" The bigger of the two guys swept his light from Cruz's face to the dragon's blood warrior, then back to Cruz. "Give us the rock, kids."

Cruz gulped hard. He couldn't just hand it over to Nebula, but what choice did he have? They were in a tight trench, hemmed in on all sides. Talk about an impossible escape.

"I'm in no mood for games," barked Nebula Number One. They heard the soft whir of a laser powering up.

"I wouldn't test him," said the bigger man. "He will use it."

Cruz didn't doubt that for a second. He tightened his left fist around the cipher. His right hand went into his pocket, his fingers finding the beak of the octopod. Did he dare? He'd never deployed the spray over his head. What if, instead of hitting the men, the peacock blue mist rained down on the three of them instead? And even if Cruz did manage to hit his target, could he get both bad guys with one shot? Not likely.

Facing the warrior, Cruz pushed the octopod against his pocket, turning slightly to show its outline first to Lani, then Sailor. Both nodded that they would be ready when the time came.

"Come on, the sooner we do this, the sooner we can get out of here," said Nebula Two. "Pry out the stone and hand it up."

Cruz hesitated. Pry?

"The dragon's blood," said Sailor, glancing at the medallion. "That's the stone they want. You know, the one we *came for*?"

Cruz's jaw dropped. Didn't these guys even know what they were after? His brain raced. Maybe not. Maybe they had no idea what the cipher looked like! It *was* possible!

"Move it!" ordered the slim man with the weapon. "Cruz, you do it. *Now*."

"All right, all right," said Cruz. "I have to move past Lani."

Lani kept looking down. Cruz followed her eyes to her curled palm, held close to her side. He mouthed "Okay" to show he understood. Stepping closer to the warrior, Cruz let the hunk of black marble fall. It landed in her palm, a seamless switch. Cruz had to let go of the octopod so he could remove the dragon's blood stone. Staring up into the unblinking eyes of the warrior, Cruz whispered, "Sorry about this." He reached for the medallion.

"Cruz, no!" cried Sailor. "Remember what Emmett and your aunt said. Not with your bare hands—"

"I'll be fine," said Cruz. His gaze met hers. "Trust me?"

Sailor shook her head, yet there was something in her eyes that said she did trust him.

Cruz tried to remove the hunk of cinnabar. He jiggled it. He twisted it. He slid his thumbnail between the rock and the setting to inch it out but succeeded only in breaking his nail. It was no use. "It won't budge!" he yelled up to the men.

"Aw, geez! Dumb kids ... hold on." The bigger man jumped into the pit. It wasn't graceful. Hitting the ground, he stumbled backward into the statue at the end of the row. They heard a crunch, though the figure didn't fall. Cruz could almost hear his aunt shriek in protest. He knew each warrior weighed more than 300 pounds. It wasn't likely that the guy could knock one over, but he could certainly damage it.

Sailor was rolling her eyes.

There wasn't enough room for everyone in the pit. Cruz leaned against the wall, while Sailor and Lani shifted back one row of soldiers to make room for Nebula's henchman. He was a bit scary-looking, especially in the spooky glow of a flashlight. His eyes were set so deep behind a pair of bushy black eyebrows, Cruz couldn't see them. Crumbs were caught in the tangle of his black beard, and he smelled like fried chicken. Skull tattoos covered his hands and wrists, disappearing into the sleeve of his black nylon jacket.

The man slapped a giant hand over the dragon's blood stone, covering the crack with his palm. He tugged and jerked, but was also unable to free the cinnabar. Muttering, he began to inspect the bolts that held the medallion's chain in place. Finally, he shouted up, "Scorpion, gimme your laser."

Cruz spotted Lani standing between the statues. Her thumb was pointing up. The girls were ready. Cruz slipped his hand back into the pocket that held the octopod. Once Nebula got what they came for, Cruz knew it was unlikely the men would let them go. If Cruz was going to do something, he'd better do it. Cruz spun the octopod in his pocket so the beak faced outward. He took a deep breath. "Team Cousteau—now!"

Cruz whirled toward the wall. He flung his right arm straight up, grabbed his right shoulder with his left hand, buried his head into the crook of his left arm, and squeezed the octopod's blue rings. He heard the *ssssssst* of mist.

There was a cry.

A burst of laser fire.

A heavy clunk.

Cruz knew he had to wait until the spray dissipated—at least 15 seconds. Once he felt it was safe, he opened his eyes. Above him, Scorpion was gone. There was a good chance he'd fallen into the fourth flank, on the other side of the wall. Next to Cruz, Scorpion's partner was out cold. Sailor stood over him, the clay arm of a warrior clutched in her hand.

"It was on the ground," she was quick to say.

For a moment, Cruz, Lani, and Sailor stared at one another as if they couldn't believe what had just happened—what they had done!

Lani finally broke the spell. "Let's go!"

They charged down the flank toward the front of the exhibit, darting through the warriors as fast as they could, which wasn't fast at all given how tightly the figures were packed. Swerving, Cruz tried to spot Mell in the air but couldn't find her.

When they reached the front row of statues, they followed the perimeter of the outer wall to the first flank. It was another sharp turn and more bobbing between soldiers to get back to the ladder. Lani, Sailor, and Cruz scampered up the rungs, flew over the rail, and scrambled back to where they'd left Emmett by the recycling bins.

He wasn't there.

"Emmett?" huffed Sailor, her own breathless voice echoing back to her.

Cruz spun. "Where is he?"

"Here's his tablet!" Lani was kneeling nearby.

Cruz shivered. Emmett would never have left this behind.

"I'm not getting *any* biosignatures now," said Sailor, checking her own tablet. "Not even from the men in the pit. Nebula has to be blocking me."

"We took out two of them," said Lani. "That leaves just one."

"Prescott," deduced Cruz. It had to be him.

A few feet beyond the tablet, they found Mell's honeycomb remote. Cruz used it to recall his honeybee drone. Cruz scanned the walkway. The only thing they were missing now was Emmett Lu.

15

▶ **"TAKE IT EASY** ... *will you?" Prescott had to use some muscle to keep a firm grip on Emmett's arm. He towed the explorer through the foyer of the museum. "Stop ... I'm on ... your side—ow!" The kid had stomped on his foot. "I work with Zebra. I'm Cobra. Did you hear me? I'm with Nebula, too."*

Emmett suddenly stopped struggling. "Too?"

"Look, I know Zebra is supposed to be your primary contact, but her cover is in jeopardy."

"Her ... cover?" squawked Emmett. "Her?"

"I need to talk to you," said Prescott. "Of course, it would have made it much easier for all of us, if I'd known you were Jaguar—"

"Me? Jaguar?"

What? Was Prescott speaking a foreign language? At least the kid had stopped fighting. Prescott released Emmett with an annoyed shove. "You can drop the act. I realize Zebra is the only one that's supposed to know your identity, but things have changed."

He watched Emmett straighten his jacket and push those crazy glasses of his up the bridge of his nose. Behind flaming red squares, brown eyes stared at Prescott with mistrust, fear, and contempt. Prescott could hardly blame him. Emmett knew who he was and what he was capable of. Prescott wouldn't have thought twice about getting rid of Emmett if he'd stood in the way of Cruz and the cipher. Of course, that was before he knew Emmett was Jaguar. Someone should have told him. Not that it would have mattered. Prescott's job was to take care of Lion's loose ends. And that's what

Jaguar would be when all of this was over. Emmett was smart to be scared, thought Prescott. Too bad it wouldn't save his life.

Emmett rubbed his upper arm. He kept looking over his shoulder at the door to the exhibit. "Uh . . . so . . . how'd you find me anyway?"

"Swan," he replied. "She told me everything. Well, not everything, but enough. Once I discovered Nebula monitors Cruz through those mood glasses of yours, I put two and two together." Prescott watched Emmett's colorful frames bleach white. A second later, the kid's face did the same. "You didn't know Zebra outfitted the glasses with a mini cam?"

"Oh yeah . . . yeah . . . sure, I knew," stuttered Emmett.

He had no clue.

Typical Nebula. Trust no one. Spy on the spy. Prescott didn't like this. Lion should never have involved a child in his schemes. Prescott wanted to ask Emmett how he'd gotten himself tangled in such a mess but thought better of it. Emmett probably had no idea what he was in for when Lion had recruited him. Now he was in over his head. Anybody could see that.

"Why can't you leave him alone?" snapped Emmett. "Do you even know what's going on? Do you know what Nebula is doing?"

"None of my business," said Prescott.

"It is so," spit Emmett. "The minute you tried to drown him in Hawaii you made it your business."

"Things aren't always black and white, kid." Pulling a holo-card from his pocket, Prescott held it out. "Here. Press your finger onto any part of the surface. The card is programmed to your print so my number will show up only for you."

"A fingerprint bio card?" Emmett flipped it.

"Text or call. You probably won't need it," said Prescott with a nod to the doors leading to the warriors. "My guys should have everything wrapped up in there by now."

Again, Emmett glanced over his shoulder. "They didn't hurt them, did they?"

Oh man, was this kid the wrong choice for a spy.

Prescott shook his head. "Emmett . . ."

The boy spun, his shoes squeaking on the tiles, and ran toward the exhibit.

"Don't get attached, Jaguar," Prescott called after him. "It's the only way to survive."

Emmett kept running, his camouflage jacket billowing out behind him.

You'll never outrun Nebula, thought Prescott.

No one ever did. And lived.

16

▶ **"IT'S MY FAULT,"** moaned Emmett for the millionth time.

And for the millionth time, Cruz responded, "It isn't."

It was Tuesday mid-morning, and they were back on board *Orion*, unpacking.

Cruz sighed. "How could you know that Zebra planted a cam the size of a speck of dust in your glasses?"

"I should have found it. It's my fault."

"It isn't." One million and one. "Besides, if it hadn't been your glasses, Nebula would have found some other way to spy on us." Cruz tossed a ball of clean socks into his open drawer like a basketball player putting up a free throw. "Remember the security cams we set up?"

"Oh yeah," mumbled Emmett. "Also my fault."

Cruz understood why his friend was bummed, but nobody blamed Emmett for what happened. Besides, it wasn't all doom and gloom. Thanks to the emoto-glasses, Prescott was on the wrong trail. He'd wrongly assumed that Emmett was Jaguar. Now they had the Nebula agent fooled *and* they had his private cell phone number! They also had another piece of the spy puzzle. They knew Zebra was a woman.

Even with the evidence against his aunt mounting, Cruz still resisted the idea that she was the spy. He couldn't believe Aunt Marisol would put a camera in Emmett's glasses. And what about their reunion at the airport? Aunt Marisol had thrown her arms around Cruz the second she laid eyes on him. She'd always been a big hugger, but this hug was different. This one was an I-was-scared-I-might-never-see-you-again squeeze.

"I confess, I was a bit worried," Aunt Marisol had told Cruz, Emmett, Sailor, and Lani as they gathered around her. "I kept telling the authorities I wasn't the woman they were looking for, but..."

As she spoke, Cruz's eyes dropped to the virtugraph cupped in his hand. The red arrow swung to point in her direction. She was telling the truth. It didn't rule her out as Zebra, of course, but it meant his aunt hadn't deliberately tried to stall their quest for the cipher. She really *had* been detained. It was enough to give Cruz doubt. And hope.

"Now we know how Nebula was always one step ahead of you." Emmett was still kicking himself. "All they had to do was tune in to me!" He looked at Cruz through a pair of square glasses the color of earthworms. The frames did nothing but sit on his face like a couple of, well, dead worms. And Cruz hated them. "Where are your emoto-glasses?"

Emmett nodded to his desk. "In the drawer. I'm running a complete diagnostic now, along with Fanchon's Hacker Tracker software. Not that it will do much good. I have a feeling Zebra covered her tracks well."

"You are going to wear them again, though, aren't you?"

"Maybe. I'm not sure what to do." Emmett began stuffing dirty clothes into his laundry bag. "If I disable the camera or remove it, Nebula will know something's up, but I can hardly keep wearing them and let them spy on us."

They'd been fortunate to escape Nebula at the Terra-Cotta Army museum. It would be dangerous to let the spies continue peeking in on their lives, especially when they were so close to completing the formula. On the other hand, if they could figure out a way to know *when* Nebula was watching, maybe it could work to their advantage...

Someone was knocking on their cabin door.

"Hi, guys!" greeted Bryndis when Emmett opened up. Sailor was with her. "You made it back just in time. Even though it's EAC week,

Professor Benedict said we had to practice our night-vision photography skills for the thylacine mission." She was talking a little too loudly. Cruz suspected it was for the benefit of Ali, who was stepping out of his cabin across the hall. "Um ... Team Cousteau is scheduled for time in the CAVE this afternoon."

"Thanks, Bryndis. That's good to know," said Emmett, his acting skills even worse.

The second Emmett shut the door, Bryndis marched over to Cruz. "I'm glad you found the seventh cipher, but what's this about you touching cinnabar?"

Cruz narrowed his eyes at Sailor, who was suddenly intent on checking her teeth in the dresser mirror.

"It was no big deal," said Cruz. "I barely touched it."

"Sailor said the cinnabar might have had some drops of liquid in it," continued Bryndis. "If that's true, when the Nebula agent or you tried to take it out of the setting, it could have released mercury vapors, exposing all three of you."

"We're all fine," Cruz assured her.

She put her hands on her hips. "How do you know? Mercury vapors are colorless and odorless."

"She's got you there," said Emmett.

"Uh ... our OS bands would have told us," said Cruz, snapping his fingers in victory.

"Unless they aren't programmed to detect mercury," countered Bryndis.

"She's got you there," echoed Sailor.

"This is nothing to mess around with," said Bryndis. "Inhaled mercury goes from the lungs into the bloodstream, where it can damage the brain and the kidneys. Did you know mercury can stay in the body for weeks or months?"

Cruz hadn't known that.

"I already told them they should go to sick bay and get checked out by Dr. Eikenboom, to be safe," said Emmett.

Bryndis glanced at Cruz's half-unpacked duffel. "Why aren't you up there right now?"

"It's really not—"

"Does your aunt know about this?"

Cruz knew a question when he heard one, and that was not a question. *That* was a threat. He put his hands up. "Okay, you win. I'll go."

"Impressive." Sailor looked at her OS band. "One minute three seconds. That's twice as long as I lasted."

"We'll get Lani on the way," said Bryndis.

Cruz hesitated. "What about our CAVE assignment?"

Bryndis spun him toward the door. "We've got time."

Crowding into the sick bay waiting room, Team Cousteau minus one didn't have to wait long to see the doctor.

"Your OS bands didn't alert us, which they would have done had any of you been exposed to anything above a normal mercury level," Dr. Eikenboom informed them.

Cruz resisted the impulse to spout, "Told ya."

"But it was wise of you to come in anyway," said the physician, which earned Cruz a look from Bryndis that said, "Told ya." The ship's doctor asked if any of the four had symptoms of mercury poisoning, like a metallic taste; nausea or vomiting; muscle weakness; problems with coordination; changes in hearing, speech, or vision; or difficulty breathing, standing, or walking straight. They didn't, but they promised to return to the medical unit if they did.

"That's good," said Dr. Eikenboom. "I'm going to run full diagnostics on your OS bands to be certain they're accurately measuring all chemicals and pollutants. Also, as a precaution, I want to get blood from each of you to test your mercury levels. I don't expect to find anything, but I want to be absolutely sure."

Cruz flinched. Blood? He had to give blood?

Back at the Academy, the Synthesis had sent lab tech Jericho Miles to get a sample of Cruz's blood. Cruz hadn't understood then what the organization was after, but he sure did now. The Synthesis wanted to see if his mom's cell-regeneration formula worked. At the time, Jericho had let Cruz off the hook and had provided the Synthesis with a sample of his own blood instead.

As before, Cruz's instincts told him not to submit to the test. Unfortunately, surrounded by his friends and unable to come up with a good excuse as to why he couldn't get jabbed, he had little choice in the matter. When it was his turn, Cruz took off his jacket and held out his arm. What else could he do? Watching the vial fill with dark red liquid, Cruz hoped nobody would discover that he was ... different.

As he walked out of sick bay, his jacket slung over his shoulder, Cruz looked from the bandage stuck on the crook of his arm to Bryndis. "Satisfied?"

"*Já.* Sorry to be so insistent. I don't want anything bad happening to you."

"I know. Thanks." Even so, Cruz *was* worried. Had he just given Nebula exactly what they'd been after?

Squeezing his other arm, Bryndis planted a kiss on his cheek. That *did* help.

AFTER LUNCH, THEY HAD A HALF HOUR before Team Cousteau was due in the CAVE for their photography assignment. While Emmett checked how the diagnostics were progressing on his emoto-glasses, Cruz finished the last of his unpacking. Cruz yanked the drawstring tight on his laundry bag and placed it next to the door for tomorrow's pickup. He zipped and folded his empty duffel back, then flung it to the top shelf on his side of the closet. All that was left was to return Emmett's hide-and-seek jacket. Cruz reached for the coat on his bed. "Hey, Em, you want to trade back?"

"Sorry ... trade what?"

"I grabbed your coat by mistake when we were in Xi'an."

Emmett turned from his computers. "No, you didn't."

"Yeah, I did."

"I don't think so." If Emmett had been wearing his emoto-frames, Cruz knew they would have been peach squares with rounded corners, signaling slight annoyance. Emmett slid back his chair and went to his side of the closet, found the hide-and-seek coat he'd hung up, and started pulling things out of the pockets: a package of baked pumpkin seeds, a compact solar charger, a stylus, a key ring with a little gold bear dangling from it that his mom had given him, another pack of seeds ...

It was Emmett's coat, all right.

"That's weird." Cruz dug into the pocket of the coat he held. "At the museum, I found this time capsule. Sailor was with me when I discovered it. She would have said if it was hers. And Lani wasn't here when we won them, so this one *has* to be yours." He held out the capsule. "But how did it get in *my* pocket?"

"You're zero for two. The capsule's not mine either." Emmett went back to his desk. He reached into his second drawer. The small purple cylinder he held between his thumb and index finger was identical to Cruz's. "See?"

They both stared at the capsule in Cruz's palm.

Taryn had given Fanchon's memory keepers to Team Cousteau as a prize for winning the scavenger hunt—one to each member. As far as they knew, they were the only explorers on board *Orion* who were in possession of them. So, if this wasn't Emmett's, Cruz's, or Sailor's, it had to belong to Dugan or Bryndis. But which one?

Cruz's roommate lifted a shoulder. "Only one way to find out."

"Should I?" Cruz hesitated. It seemed wrong to watch someone's memory without their permission.

"How else can you return it?"

He had a point.

"Okay, but I'm watching for only as long as it takes me to figure out whose it is," said Cruz.

Emmett wiggled his eyebrows. "I'm betting on Bryndis."

Curling his fingers around the capsule, Cruz took a deep breath. He shut his eyelids. Viewing the world through the eyes of the capsule's owner, Cruz found himself strolling down one of the ship's hallways. It reminded him of the one on the fourth deck. His head turned—or rather, the capsule's owner's head turned—and he saw a door labeled TECHNOLOGY LAB. It *was* the fourth deck! He saw the quick flick of a wrist and the flash of a tiny black card. Instead of OS bands, *Orion*'s faculty, staff, and crew used cards or biometrics to access certain areas of the ship. Cruz was confused. If he was seeing Bryndis's or Dugan's memory, where did one of them get an access card? And why didn't he or she use their OS band? Cruz was now inside the lab. Rather than waiting for Fanchon or Dr. Vanderwick, as the explorers were instructed to do, he found himself easily weaving through the maze of cubicles to the back of the compartment. He was in front of a door. Cruz would certainly never forget *this* door. The merry-go-lab!

The hand tapping in the code looked familiar . . .

4-2-9-2-4-4.

Not a single scratch, chip, or mark on the cherry red nails.

Could it be . . .

Taryn?

Cruz was staring into an iris scanner. The blue beam shut off, and the door was opening.

He could see right away that *this* was no storage room. Cruz was moving into a brightly lit lab. To his left, he saw racks of clear drawers filled with electronic parts: cables, circuit boards, processors, cards, and such. On his right was a wall made up of about a dozen screens. The top two rows of computers were running programs, while the bottom row of screens was dark.

Fanchon came toward him, tying on a zebra-print head scarf. "Hey!"

"Sorry to be a bother."

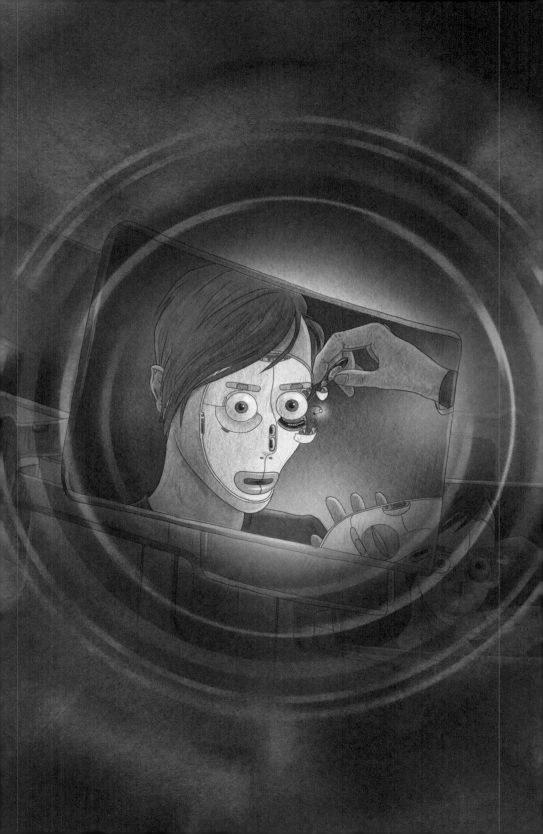

Cruz instantly knew the voice ringing in his ears. It *was* Taryn! Cruz was reliving a memory from his adviser. The capsule belonged to Taryn.

"You're never a bother," answered Fanchon. "What's up?"

"My left eye again."

"Still twitching?"

"Yes, and people are starting to notice. I have a feeling Monsieur Legrand thinks I am flirting with him."

Hearing her again, Cruz felt a lump rise in his throat.

Fanchon was laughing. "Okay, let's have a look." Looming close, the tech lab chief gently tapped around Taryn's upper check and temple. What was she doing? Cruz heard several clicks and an odd whirring sound. Fanchon was lifting something away from Taryn's face. She set it down on the counter. Oh, a mask! This must be from last Halloween or something. Taryn was probably trying on different costumes. The disguise sure was lifelike: a turned-up nose, pink lips, smooth pale skin . . .

Whoa! This was no mask.

This. Was. Taryn's. Face.

Cruz's head was turning again. He caught his reflection in one of the dark computer screens on the wall. "Arrrrrgh!" His eyelids flew open.

Emmett was in front of him. "What's wrong? What happened?"

"I saw . . . She was . . . I can't . . ."

"Cruz, you're freaking out and you're freaking me out," squeaked Emmett. "What happened? What did you see?"

"T-Taryn," he coughed.

Emmett nodded. "You saw Taryn. What was she doing?"

"No . . . I *was* Taryn." Cruz put a hand to his forehead. It was on fire.

"It's her time capsule. Emmett, she's a . . . I mean, she *was* . . . a . . . robot!"

17

"YOU MUST HAVE misinter-

preted the memory," reasoned Emmett.

"How do you misinterpret someone taking off *their face*?" hissed Cruz.

They were walking briskly down the main deck passage on their way to the CAVE. The pair was early for their session, but after the shock of the time capsule, Cruz needed to get out of their cabin for some fresh air.

"Besides, it wasn't a dream," said Cruz. "It was a memory—Taryn's memory. She must have put the capsule in my pocket at the Tiger's Nest. But why? What was she trying to tell me?"

Emmett thought for a minute. "Maybe nothing. Maybe all she wanted was for you to know who she was."

"I...I guess." Cruz still couldn't believe it. His beloved adviser: a robot?

Reaching the CAVE door, they held up to wait for Bryndis, Sailor, Lani, and Dugan. It was a rule that you always entered and left the virtual reality compartment as a team.

Looking back, Cruz realized he had missed some hints about their adviser along the way. He recalled the day *Orion* had set sail. Standing next to Taryn at the rail, waving to his dad, Cruz had asked her if anyone had come to see her off. "Nope," she'd replied. "Free as a bird." Another time she'd told the explorers they were her only family. Then there were her bright green eyes. Cruz had only seen such a color in one other place: bobbing in a glass globe in the tech lab.

Emmett was tapping him. "Remember our last Funday when Taryn announced we were doing robotics and everybody cheered? She was happy that we were happy. Now we know why."

They sure did.

"She loved the Planet Pup companion your group made for Hubbard," continued Emmett. "That was a good idea."

"Yeah." Cruz grinned. "Except it took us forever to iron out the bugs. Thank goodness for Fan— Emmett, *Fanchon*! Couldn't Fanchon repair Taryn?"

"Sure," said Emmett. "Unless she was too damaged or something."

Cruz's brain was reeling. "Just after we got back from Bhutan, Fanchon went to Washington, D.C., remember? For her annual evaluation with Dr. Hightower. What if that was a cover story? What if she really went to repair Taryn?"

"It's possible, I guess—"

"But why wouldn't she tell us?"

"Probably couldn't," said Emmett. "If it was a top secret project for the Synthesis ..."

"I've got to go talk to her—"

"She still won't be able to tell you," broke in Emmett. "What's changed?"

"This!" Cruz brought out the time capsule in his pocket. "Once she knows I know, she'll have to tell me."

"I wouldn't be so sure."

"Fanchon wouldn't lie to me." Dropping his backpack in the corner of the passage next to the CAVE entrance, Cruz began to walk back down the passage. "Not to *me*."

"What makes you think— Hold on, you're going *now*?" Emmett gulped. "We're starting in ten minutes, Cruz. We'll miss our slot—"

"We won't." Cruz whirled, calling over his shoulder, "I'll be back in time." Charging up the stairs, he met Dugan and Lani coming down.

"Hey, where are you—" started Dugan.

"Be right back. I've got ten minutes."

"More like nine!" Dugan shouted after him.

Cruz charged up three flights of steps to the fourth deck. Throwing his wrist against the security panel, he practically skidded into the tech lab. "Fanchon! Are you here? Fanchon!"

A lemur-print head scarf popped around the corner of a nearby cubicle. "Cruz?" Fanchon pushed up her safety goggles. "What's up?"

He didn't have time to say it slowly, politely, or delicately.

"Taryn..." panted Cruz. "She's...a...robot, isn't she?"

Fanchon's eyes grew almost as wide as those of the lemurs clinging to her skull. "What?"

"I have to...know," he pleaded. "I've got five minutes...due in the CAVE."

The tech lab chief rolled the stool she was sitting on out of the cubicle. "You think Taryn is—was—a robot?"

"Is she?"

"A robot?" She frowned. "No, Cruz. No. I can't even imagine where such rumors get started, though I suppose with twenty-four explorers living on a ship I really shouldn't be surprised by anything."

"So you didn't...go to Academy headquarters...to repair her?"

"Where in the world did you hear such a thing?"

Still breathing hard, Cruz held out his right hand to show her the capsule. "Taryn told me."

Fanchon tried not to change expression, but it was too late. He'd seen the quick intake of breath. She had not expected *this*. He had one more surprise. Cruz stretched out his left arm, uncurling his fingers. In his palm was the virtugraph. The black needle pointed at Fanchon.

Without a word, Cruz turned. And ran.

Fanchon may have called after him. He wasn't sure. Had she forgotten he had the virtugraph? Cruz was angry, but mostly he was hurt. He had never expected her to outright lie to him—not about someone... something—as important as Taryn.

Blinking back tears, Cruz flew down one staircase after the other.

He made it to the CAVE with less than a minute to spare.

"Cutting it awfully close, Cruz," said Dugan.

"Sorry." He wiped his eyes.

Emmett's gaze was burning a hole into his brain, but all Cruz could do was give him a quick head shake. The full story would have to wait.

Dugan waved his OS band in front of the security panel, the door slid aside, and in went Team Cousteau. In the time it took for the compartment door to close, the six explorers were transported to a rocky alpine slope. They had a 360-degree view of jagged peaks rising above forested hillsides. Overhead, the setting sun tinted cirrus clouds a rosy pink, while a brisk wind fluttered their hair. The sparse vegetation on the mountainside included ferns, sedges, and clumps of grasses, while a thick blanket of compact cushion plants, cranberries, and club mosses covered the ground.

Professor Benedict appeared before them in holo form. "Welcome, Team Cousteau. You are in the Hartz Mountains in Tasmania, where the most recent thylacine video was taken. Please hike along the wooden boardwalk to the lake, then find a spot to settle in for your evening shoot. Most of the animals that live here are nocturnal, so this will give you a good opportunity to hone your observation skills and practice your night photography. You're likely to see wallabies, possums, platypus, pademelon, echidnas, and more! Take photos of what you see, then upload them to our class account by tomorrow morning. The sunrise will signal your time is up. Good luck, explorers!" Pixel by pixel, their instructor vanished.

Team Cousteau set out, tramping single file along the creaky boardwalk. As they descended in elevation, they moved through a subalpine zone dotted with pines, gangly eucalyptus trees, and small shrubs. Finally, they reached a dense lowland forest. It was dark by the time they found the lake, but a pale yellow full moon lit the area.

"Nobody said anything about a five-mile hike!" said Emmett, wiggling out of his pack.

Bryndis reached for her water bottle. "I bet it was Monsieur Legrand's idea. He did say he was going to get us in better shape."

"I'm dog tired," said Dugan, dropping to his knees.

"Woof!" Sailor slapped him on the back. "This is no time for a nap."

"Everybody, let's spread out," suggested Lani. "That way we'll be able to take photos of different animals."

Cruz stopped to take a few swigs from his water bottle before continuing down the boardwalk. He wanted to find a spot on the shore of the lake. He felt he was more likely to see wildlife there since water attracted animals. It wasn't long before Cruz came upon a tiny stream that fed into the lake. Perfect! To make himself less noticeable, he crouched near a fallen tree. He slid his MC camera onto his head, popping the lens down over one eye. He leaned both arms on the stump, then set his chin on his forearms. Cruz watched. And waited. The shimmer of moonlight on the water was making him drowsy. He was starting to fall asleep when he heard rustling.

Two dark eyes were peering into his lens! It looked like a large rat. As the animal ventured closer, Cruz could make out a pair of small rounded ears, tan fur with white polka dots, and a long tail. Cruz's camera identified it as spotted-tail quoll. Cruz took several photos of the little guy slurping water.

"Emmett Lu to Cruz Coronado."

Cruz hit his comm pin. "Cruz, here," he whispered.

"How's your count?"

"One quoll." Cruz yawned. "You?"

"A big zero. I scared a frog and sat on an anthill."

Cruz laughed.

"Where are you?" asked Emmett.

"About a hundred yards down the boardwalk."

"I might come down there if it doesn't pick up soon. It's crickets up here. Not literally."

"Take a right at the fork where it cuts around the lake," Cruz directed him. "I'm at the first log on the left. Follow the stream. If you were wearing your emoto-glasses, I could see you."

"If I was wearing my emoto-glasses, Nebula could see *you*. Emmett, out."

Craaaaawwww!

The screech of an owl made Cruz nearly rocket out of his boots. Once his pulse calmed, Cruz began to scan the branches above him using his telephoto lens. He moved inch by inch but couldn't locate the animal. Talk about frustrating.

Craaaaawwww!

"I know you're up there somewhere," he muttered. "I'll find you ..."

Cruz's neck was sore from being scrunched into his shoulders turtle-like, and something sharp was digging into his hip. Now he understood why Professor Benedict wanted them to practice. Just because you have all the right equipment doesn't mean the photography is going to be easy or comfortable...

Or dry. His foot was wet.

Cruz heard movement in the brush behind him. "Emmett, over here," he whispered. He felt someone kneel beside him. "I keep hearing an owl, but I can't seem to—"

"Up in that pine—about ten o'clock."

The gravelly voice sent a shudder through Cruz. He flipped his MC camera up so hard that the whole thing flew off his head. Cruz stared at the man in the fishing hat, vest, and flannel shirt beside him. "D-Dr. Fallowfeld?"

"I know," the scientist said quietly. "I've got to stop ambushing you in your virtual-reality scenarios."

"I...you..." Cruz had not expected this. Not here and certainly not now. He had tons of questions to ask his mother's colleague, but suddenly he couldn't think of a single one. His brain had gone blank.

"I don't have much time," said Dr. Fallowfeld. The moonlight seemed to carve the burn scars deeper into his face. "I got your message. What do you need?"

Cruz leaned back so he could reach the virtugraph in his pocket. Bringing it out, he pressed the dove in with his thumb to activate the instrument. "I'm trying to understand something. Why did you lie to me back at the Academy?"

"Direct." He snorted. "I like that. I didn't lie ... Well, I did, but not about the things that mattered, Cruz. Not about how your mom died or Nebula. I wanted to get you on a plane home, to safety, and it was the quickest way I knew to do it. I admit, I was less than candid about my role in your mom's work, but the more you knew, the more danger you were in."

"So you *did* help my mom with her research?"

"Only by testing some of the components. She did the bulk of the work. I never saw the full formula. That's the truth. Of course, I doubt Nebula would believe that. If they knew I was still alive ... If they knew I was on board *Orion* ..."

Cruz glanced down to see which arrow on the virtugraph was pointing toward Dr. Fallowfeld. It was too dark. He could see only shadows.

"What are you doing?" Dr. Fallowfeld drew back, suspicious. "What is that?"

"A compass," replied Cruz. "I'm supposed to ... uh ... make sure I don't stray off course. Can you tell me about the serum?"

"You mean how it will affect *you*?"

"Then you know ...?"

"That you were exposed, yes. Beyond that, beyond confirming that you possess accelerated cell regeneration, there's little more I can tell you. As I said, I only worked on a small portion of the project. Your mother kept a detailed logbook of her work." He tugged on the brim of his fishing hat. "After I got out of the hospital, I tried to find it, but it had disappeared from the lab's vault. I am sure the Synthesis has it, or maybe Nebula by now."

Cruz kept silent. He'd be breaking his promise to the Archive to tell the scientist where the logbook was.

"I'm surprised the Synthesis hasn't been after you," said Dr. Fallowfeld. "The only thing I can figure is that they are biding their time, waiting for you to find all the pieces of the cipher."

"The cipher?" Cruz's head snapped up. "You know about that, too?"

"Know about it?" He managed a slight grin. "It was my idea. Nebula was closing in. Engraving the stone and splitting it into pieces seemed the best way to get Petra out of Washington, D.C., *and* hide the formula. Of course, we underestimated the lengths Nebula would go to to silence us. None of us ever dreamed that Hezekiah Brume ..." He dipped his head. "I am sorry about what happened to your mother, Cruz. And even sorrier that I couldn't prevent it."

Cruz nodded.

"There's a lot we still don't know about the formula." Dr. Fallowfeld put a hand to his cratered face. "You might be the only person in the world, Cruz, who can say they have the potential to live forever. That's an incredible gift. And curse."

Cruz did not need to ask what he meant. He knew. Life *was* a gift. But everlasting life?

He had already lost his mother. Cruz knew that, one by one, he would lose each of the people that mattered most to him: his father, Aunt Marisol, Lani, Emmett, Sailor, Bryndis . . . and on and on and on . . .

An orange ribbon of light was peeking through the trees. "The sun's coming up," said Dr. Fallowfeld. "I must go. I won't be in touch again, Cruz. It's too dangerous—"

"Wait!" In a few more minutes, Cruz would be able to read the virtugraph. "Once I complete the cipher, will Mom's journal tell me to bring it to you?"

"I . . . I'm not sure. She did that all on her own. There were some things I wanted her to keep secret, in case Nebula ever got to me."

"But you could do it, right? You could re-create my mother's serum."

"I can't, Cruz," said Dr. Fallowfeld.

"Why not? You're the only one I know who can—"

"It's not that I don't want to. I *can't*. Nobody can."

Cruz was getting frustrated. "I don't know what you mean."

"One of the components of your mom's serum is a toxin from a South American frog."

"Okay." He was still lost.

"I'm sorry, Cruz, I only found out myself a short time ago—"

"What?"

"The frog . . . it went extinct last year."

Cruz felt the compass slip from his fingers.

18

"HE'S LYING," said Lani.

"He's wrong," said Emmett.

"He's lying *and* he's wrong," said Sailor.

Sprawled out on his bed, Cruz flung an arm over his face. Solving difficult clues, searching high and low, running from Nebula, risking their lives—had it all been for nothing?

"If the frog really *is* extinct, there might be another toxin from a similar frog or even another animal that can be substituted." Emmett looked up from his tablet. "This article from the World Toxin Bank says a single animal's venom is made up of dozens or even hundreds of different toxins."

Cruz peered over the top of his forearm. "There's a World Toxin Bank?"

"Yep! They collect and store toxins from animals all over the world so that researchers can study them for use in human medications. More than a hundred thousand species of animals are known to be toxic: scorpions, spiders, ants, bees, wasps, lizards, jellyfish, anemones, sea urchins, sea stars, leeches, fish, and *frogs*—to name a few."

"Crikey!" Sailor was reading over his shoulder. "It says here there are millions of toxins in nature that we *still* have yet to discover. That could be a fun career. Venom wrangler."

Dr. Fallowfeld had said he'd only worked on a small portion of the serum. Maybe the toxin he was talking about wasn't critical to the formula. Or, like Emmett said, perhaps, another toxin could be used in its place. Lani and Sailor could also be right. In the darkness of the CAVE, Cruz had been unable to read the virtugraph. Dr. Fallowfeld could have been lying to try to convince him to quit searching for the cipher. In her journal, Cruz's mother had warned him about trusting anyone with the Synthesis.

Lani was shaking her head. "We're getting ahead of ourselves. Let's focus on completing the cipher; then we'll follow Cruz's mom's instructions on what to do with it—"

"I bet she's going to tell you to take it to Dr. Fallowfeld like you thought," Emmett said. "That's the logical conclusion. If he *was* working on the formula, he'd know the most about it."

"Unless Mom feared Nebula might kill him," said Cruz. "Or she didn't trust him."

"I still think he's lying," grumbled Sailor.

"You guys!" Lani hung over the side of the chair. "Cruz, maybe your mom will direct you to take it to Dr. Fallowfeld, but *maybe* she won't. Maybe the formula won't work the way it's written, but *maybe* it will. Can't we take it one step at a time?"

Lani was right. There were too many possibilities, too many outcomes. Worrying about what could happen instead of what was happening wasn't going to get Cruz anywhere.

Cruz grinned at his best friend. "One step at a time."

Propping himself up onto his elbow, Cruz saw that the message icon on his tablet was blinking. He tapped the blue envelope to open it:

Meet me on the fourth-level bow deck at 8 p.m.
Tell no one. Come alone.
You won't need the virtugraph. I promise.
　　　—FQ

"Captain Iskandar says we're ahead of schedule," said Sailor. "We'll be in Hobart tomorrow night. Guess we should open the journal tonight, then, huh?"

"T-tonight?" stammered Cruz.

"I can't," said Lani. "Nyomie snagged me for my evaluation. But you can all go ahead and I'll catch up when I'm done—"

"No," Cruz said quickly. "We'll wait until we can open it together, like we've always done it. We'll do it after we get back from the mission."

"Peachy." Sailor hopped to her feet. "Got to go. I've still got to upload my photos from the CAVE photo shoot."

"Did you get anything good?" asked Cruz.

"A possum, a sugar glider, and"—Sailor crossed her eyes—"a thylacine. So much for virtual *reality*. This mission is going to be so boring."

"You're going to have to eat those words when we see a thylacine," said Emmett.

Sailor grunted. "Emmett, if we find a thylacine, I'll eat one of your stinky socks!"

"DAD!"

"Hi, son." Hearing his father's easy voice always calmed Cruz.

It was 7:30 in the evening back home and 4:30 in the afternoon on board *Orion*. However, because they were on opposite sides of the international date line, the pair was almost a full day apart. Off the eastern coast of Australia, *Orion* was 21 hours ahead of Kauai.

"I just had an interesting conversation with Pendrina Antonov," said his father.

"Dad, it's okay. I touched a small piece of cinnabar ... uh ... while I was getting the seventh cipher." He figured it was best to skip over the part about Nebula being there, too. "But only for a second. I'm all right, honest."

"I know. Pendrina told me that Dr. Eikenboom gave you, Lani, and Sailor a thorough once-over and you're all fine—no trace of mercury was measured by your OS band or found in your bloodstream. However, I was surprised that your aunt didn't mention it to me."

"That's because she ... uh ... doesn't exactly know."

His father's head tilt told Cruz that he'd already come to that conclusion. "Anything else you want to tell me that your aunt doesn't know?"

"N-no?"

His dad gave him a skeptical smirk.

"I did want to ask you something," said Cruz. "Did you know Dr. Fallowfeld very well?"

"Elistair? Um .... a little. Why?" He loomed close to the camera. "He's been to see you again, hasn't he?"

Cruz related his encounter with Dr. Fallowfeld in the CAVE. "It's not going to keep me from searching for the last piece of the cipher, but I thought you might be able to tell me if he's trustworthy."

"I met him once or twice, but that's about it. Your mom didn't talk much about her colleagues at the Synthesis, and because her work was classified, I learned not to ask questions. Up until Elistair showed up at the Academy six months ago to find you, I had no idea where he was or even if he was still alive." He ran his hand through his thick hair. "I can't tell you whether or not to trust him, son, but I can say that if more people at the Synthesis had supported your mom, things might have turned out very differently for her, and us. I'd be wary, if I were you."

"Thanks, Dad. That's helpful."

"How's everything else going?"

"Great." Cruz told his dad about the thylacine mission. He also showed him the canvas of Hubbard that Bryndis had painted for him. "She's a good friend."

"Maybe a little more than a friend, huh?"

Warmth flooded Cruz's cheeks. "Maybe."

"Anytime you want to talk about anything girl-related ... I'm here."

He rolled his eyes. "I know."

Cruz heard sleigh bells jingle, which meant someone was coming into the Goofy Foot. "I've got a customer," confirmed his dad. "Call you later! Love you, son."

"Love you, too, Dad. Bye."

It was almost time to meet Fanchon. Cruz gave Emmett an excuse about walking Hubbard and stopping by the dining room for a snack. Chef Kristos always left out a bowl of fruit, nuts, and sunflower seeds for the explorers to munch on in the evenings.

Emmett was glued to his computers. "Bring me an apple?"

"Okay."

"And some corn chips, if they have them."

"Okay."

"And those little granola snack bars but not the ones with the raisins ..."

Cruz shut the door. He'd be bringing back a whole tray of food if he stuck around much longer.

Up on the fourth level, Cruz slid aside the deck door and felt the cooling rush of the sea wind. It was a cloudy night. Globe lights strung along the V-shaped rail and the lights from the bridge one level up bathed the empty deck in a soft glow. He knew why Fanchon had chosen to meet here. Steps from the tech lab, the cozy deck was rarely used. The explorers preferred to gather on the larger outside decks on the third level of the ship, or head to the observation deck. The crew and staff usually hung out on the bridge or stern decks.

Cruz wrapped his hands around the rail, the cold metal sending a shiver through him. He watched the point of the ship's bow slice through the waters of the Tasman Sea. The up-and-down motion of the surf was hypnotic, and it took a while for Cruz, who was lost in his thoughts, to look up. When he finally did, Fanchon was beside him. One side of her face was gold, while the other side was lost in shadow. She wasn't wearing a head scarf, and the night breeze puffed up her crop of curls like caramel-coated popcorn. "It's a top secret project." Fanchon pulled a red-and-pink-striped cardigan tighter around her. "I'm sorry about lying ... You caught me by surprise ... I should have known Taryn would find a way to tell you. She's full of surprises, that girl."

Cruz wrinkled his brow. "You mean robot."

"I prefer the term 'cybernetic,'" she said. "'Secliff' is short for 'Sentient Emotive Cybernetic Life-Form.'"

"And Taryn?"

"She is Model Twenty-A, serial number eighteen twenty-five four-teen. Correspond the numbers with the letters of alphabet and the series spells 'Taryn.'"

Clever!

"Taryn was more than an autonomous machine carrying out human instructions," explained Fanchon. "I programmed her to think, feel, respond, and learn from her experiences. There's one thing you need to understand, Cruz. I may have built and named her, but she established her own identity."

"Why couldn't we know?" wondered Cruz. "We all like using the new technology that Dr. Vanderwick and you invent."

"Originally, Taryn *was* designed to assist in the lab," said Fanchon, "but, like I said, she developed her own sense of self—likes and dislikes, passions and pursuits. Early on, I saw how much she enjoyed being around the explorers. It was clear that was where she belonged, not in a lab. I asked Dr. Hightower to let her interact more with the students, and she agreed. Taryn passed each one of my tests, if you want to call it that. She was kind, caring, nurturing, yet firm and authoritative when she needed to be. She studied and got her psychology degree on her own. When an adviser position opened up, Taryn applied, and Dr. Hightower hired her." Fanchon sighed. "She didn't have to. She knew what Taryn was. But Dr. Hightower said she was, by far, the best candidate for the job. She said it wasn't fair to deny the job to her because of her ... differences. I remember that's just how she said it, too."

"That's nice," said Cruz. "But it doesn't answer my question."

"Patience, please." Exhaling, Fanchon tipped her head back to study the moonless sky. It took her a moment to go on. "Do you ever think about what makes the Academy and the Society special?"

"We're ... uh ... more curious?" That sounded too simple. "I ... I don't really know," confessed Cruz. "All I've ever wanted to do was come to the Academy. I knew it would be hard, but I guess that's why I wanted to come. To do things I couldn't do back home. And to find out what I *could* do." He knew he was rambling, but she seemed in no hurry to interrupt him. She was letting him find his answer. "My mom always said being an explorer opened up the world to her. She said it changed her life. Maybe I'm hoping it will change mine, too."

"Mmm-hmm. Facing your fears and pushing your limits, yes, that's what the Academy and the Society are all about. It's the only way to make progress. We go to the edge of what others say is possible, and we leap into the impossible." She turned to him. "The work we are doing in artificial intelligence is beyond what anyone ever imagined. Everything we know, everything we are still learning, is proving these life-forms are safe, efficient, intelligent beings, and that they have as much to contribute to the world as any human. Perhaps more.

"You see, cybernetic life-forms can and do experience the feelings that tend to promote negative behaviors, things like greed, jealousy, and laziness, but unlike us, they will rarely act on them. They view these things as counterproductive. Why would you take more than you need? Or pollute an ocean when you require the fish it sustains to survive? The fact is cybernetics is still a controversial subject. The world, as a whole, isn't ready to embrace the technology. We are trying to respect that, even as we jump forward."

Cruz resisted the impulse to again ask her where all this was leading.

Folding her hands, Fanchon rested them on the rail. "The Academy requests a great deal from your parents. We ask them to send you away to travel the world with us, to put your education, happiness, health, development—your lives—in our hands."

Now Cruz was beginning to see where she was going. "And some of our parents might not understand if one of those people wasn't actually a person," he said.

"I wish things were different. Maybe someday, when people aren't so intimidated by the technology. But not now. Not yet."

"Are you saying ...?" He took in a sharp breath. "I mean, you did repair her, didn't you?"

Her face softened. "What do you think?"

He knew it! Taryn wasn't dead. Was that the right word for it?

"After what happened at the Tiger's Nest, or what people thought happened, we had to keep up the deception," said Fanchon. "We had to act as if she was human. We transported her back to Washington, D.C., and I took things from there."

He'd been right! That's why Fanchon had gone to Academy headquarters.

"Where is she now?" Cruz was eager to know.

"Cruz . . . I . . . I'm sorry, that is one thing I cannot reveal."

"Please, Fanchon," he begged. "She died protecting me. I won't tell anybody—not my dad or aunt, not even Emmett, Sailor, or Lani. I won't tell *anyone*. I swear it."

"No." Her lips were drawn into a thin line.

Cruz deflated. How could she tell him everything but where Taryn was? It was more than unfair. It was cruel.

"Isn't it enough to know she's alive?" asked the tech lab chief.

Cruz wanted to say yes, but he couldn't. "Would she know me? Or did you—"

"She'd know you," said Fanchon. "But she wouldn't approach you. She understands what's at stake. I had to alter her physical appearance, and she has a new name, of course, but her core processor—her brain—is intact. Her memories are all there. I thought about deleting those things. I wondered if it might make it easier for her, but it didn't seem fair. She had a right to know and own her past, as we all do."

Cruz was out of questions. Taryn wasn't gone, but he would never be able to see or talk to her, wouldn't even know her if she walked past him. Maybe she already had. That was the worst part—wondering if she already had.

That night, Cruz's conversation with Fanchon kept him awake long after he should have been asleep. It was a miracle. Mr. Rook's horrible deeds at the Tiger's Nest had, in a way, been undone. Nebula hadn't won, after all.

Taryn *was* alive. Breathing. Living. Being. And that was enough.

It would have to be.

GOOD EVENING, *explorer!*

We have arrived in Hobart, the capital of Tasmania, Australia! Please report dockside tomorrow morning at 7 a.m. We'll be spending two nights on the island, camping in Hartz Mountains National Park. Prepare for cloudy and rainy (and possibly windy) weather with highs in the 60s and overnight lows in the 40s. I think it was Meriwether Lewis who once said a wise explorer always brings extra socks. Or maybe it was me! In either case, please do so.

Dare to explore,
Prof. C. Ishikawa

Cruz heard the pop of a twig on the trail behind him, but that wasn't what made him turn. It was the tiny frustrated sigh that followed. He glanced back. "You okay?"

"*Já.*" Bryndis flicked a strand of pale blond hair out of her eyes. "I've got one angry blister happening on my ankle. That's what I get for breaking in a new pair of boots."

Cruz knew how she felt. He didn't have a blister, but he could use a rest. They'd been hiking for more than three hours, pausing only once for water and snacks.

Earlier that morning, as the explorers and faculty had boarded the Auto Auto electric SUVs for the hour-and-a-half drive from Hobart, everyone had been bubbling with energy. They were in Tasmania at last! Even though their teachers had repeatedly cautioned them that a thylacine sighting would be improbable, it was hard not to hope that they might be the ones to see an animal long thought to be extinct.

Several miles inside the park, the caravan had pulled off the two-lane dirt road into a circular clearing. Piling out of the vehicles, they'd met up with wildlife biologist Nick Downing, one of the experts who'd viewed the thylacine drone video Professor Luben had shown them in class.

The athletic, stubble-faced man, who looked to be about Fanchon's age, wore a faded tan safari hat, a chestnut brown long-sleeved thermal tee, knee-length khaki hiking shorts, woolly red socks, and boots. Dr. Downing welcomed each of them with a protein bar and a viselike handshake. "Good to have you here," he said with an accent similar to Sailor's. "We're looking forward to seeing what your mobile bots will reveal. Shall we get along? We've got a ways to go."

With the biologist as their guide, they'd begun their trek through the rolling lowland forest. The path wasn't steep, but it was rocky and winding. It was also not well traveled, forcing them to divert around fallen branches or crawl over logs encrusted with mosses, mushrooms, and lichens. Near the front of the group, Cruz tried to keep up with the brisk pace set by the bulging calf muscles of their guide. A fog was beginning to close in, swallowing the tops of the trees. Cruz felt the mist condensing on his skin.

They were stopping. At last!

Ahead, Dr. Downing was leaning against a tall eucalyptus. Professor Ishikawa, who'd been hiking directly behind him, was waving everyone in. "We're in the approximate area where the dragonfly drone took the video of the thylacine," said Professor Ishikawa. "We'll have lunch here, then break into our teams to begin deploying the SHOT-bots."

"I'm starving," Emmett said to his teammates.

"Me too," said Dugan.

Sailor nodded, even as she gulped water.

Cruz happily dumped his pack. Having to bring more clothes and attaching his sleeping bag to his pack had added both weight and bulk to the load. Monsieur Legrand's practice hikes had not included these extras, and Cruz's back was feeling it. He leaned left, then right, stretching out his muscles.

Throwing a tarp on the ground, Monsieur Legrand put out trays of pocket bread and assorted meats, cheeses, and veggies for them to make their own pitas. Cruz filled a wheat pita with slices of turkey, tomatoes, and pickles, topping it with a squirt of mayo. He took a seat next to Bryndis on a half-split log. She had her boot off, her right foot resting on her left knee and her sock rolled down to her toes.

He could see the back of her ankle was red and raw. She was riffling through her pack.

"Need a bandage?" asked Cruz.

"*Já*, please."

"Aunt Marisol always has a supply of them. Hold this?" A second after Cruz handed Bryndis his sandwich, he heard her stomach rumble. "You can have it."

"No, I can't take your—"

"I can make another one," Cruz said.

She gave him a weak grin. "Thanks."

By the time Cruz came back with the bandage, Bryndis had downed half the sandwich. She *was* hungry! Cruz built a second pita, this time adding cheddar cheese and sprouts. The pocket bread was bursting.

"*Oh, mon Dieu, Cruz!*" said Monsieur Legrand.

"Too much?" Cruz reached for the tongs. "I'll put some back—"

"No, no. It's all right." His instructor patted his shoulder. "You're burning a lot of calories hiking. Plus, you've been doing some growing."

He'd thought so! Cruz stuck out a leg to show his instructor the space between his pant leg and sock. "I was thinking maybe Laundry had shrunk my pants." He had been planning to ask Nyomie to order him another pair. "How much do you think I've—"

"A good two inches, I'd say."

Cruz wondered if Aunt Marisol had noticed his growth spurt, too.

When Cruz returned with his pita, Bryndis laughed. "Now *that* is a sandwich!"

After they finished lunch, Professor Ishikawa issued their instructions. "Each team has been assigned three Soft Heliomorphic Observational Traveling robots. Fanchon and Dr. Vanderwick have designed the bots to resemble *Urtica incisa,* commonly known as stinging nettle." He held up a trio of young plants about five inches high sprouting from a mossy base. The plants had rough leaves with toothy edges and sprigs of tiny yellow flowers. "Look closely and you'll see trichomes, or little hairs, on the leaves and stems," said their teacher.

"The tips break off when they're brushed against, revealing needlelike tubes that poke the skin and cause an itching, burning rash. Be careful when handling these. They may not be real but their effects are."

The explorers knew that when programming the transmutational soft silicon casings, Fanchon and Dr. Vanderwick did their best to precisely mimic plants or fungi that were unappealing to most animals. The idea was to discourage wildlife from getting too close to the state-of-the art mobile cameras. Of course, there was never a guarantee that something wouldn't happen. The bots could—and had—gotten stepped on, sat on, munched on, and pawed at, not to mention getting tangled in bushes, stuck in mud, dunked in lakes, snagged in fishing lines, and swept away by swift river currents. It's why, wherever they went, they usually deployed several SHOT-bots.

"About a quarter mile ahead are several diverging trails," said Professor Ishikawa. "Each team will branch out on a different trail for approximately five miles. You'll deploy your first SHOT-bot, then set up camp for the night. You'll continue on your way tomorrow, walking another twenty miles and activating your two remaining SHOT-bots along the way. We will all meet at the rendezvous coordinates the following day and head back to the ship."

Since they were behind schedule, Monsieur Legrand had made the assignments. "Team Galileo, you will be led by Professor Luben and Professor Ishikawa," he said. "Team Earhart, you will go with Professor Coronado and Dr. Downing. Team Magellan, you are traveling with Professor Benedict and myself. Team Cousteau, you are in Professor Modi's capable hands."

The explorers packed up their gear and found their respective leaders. Cruz and his teammates lined up behind Professor Modi. When he reached the first intersecting path, Professor Modi raised his carved black locust wood walking stick to signal they were about to splinter off from the group. Team Cousteau headed west.

Cruz was glad that their instructor didn't go quite as fast as Dr. Downing. As they hiked, the path grew steeper, the outcrops more prominent. They trekked passed angular walls of gray dolerite rock with flecks of glittering white crystals. The trail dipped, and when it opened into a grassy meadow, Professor Modi declared they had reached the five-mile mark. "Let's deploy and camp here," he declared. "Cruz and Lani, why don't you do the first bot? Tomorrow, Bryndis and Emmett, you'll do the second, and Dugan and Sailor, you'll take the third."

Lani leaned toward Cruz. "Mind if I handle the bot? I've never done one before."

"It's all yours," said Cruz. "I'll run the diagnostic."

Putting on a pair of protective gloves, Lani carefully lifted the prickly SHOT-bot from its container. She set it on the most level spot she could find. Cruz logged in to the software on his tablet. The device had been preprogrammed. He remotely switched it on, then checked to make sure the camera and motion detector were functioning properly. He was staring at a live shot of Lani's foot. "All systems go."

"Excellent," said Professor Modi. "Send it on its way whenever you're ready. Have it travel about a mile from our location. Who knows? We might pick up something overnight. While you finish, I'll start setting up camp." He headed into the clearing.

Cruz glanced at his teammates, his finger poised above the start icon on his screen. "Here we go!"

Lani raised her hand. "Shouldn't we give it a name or something?"

"I don't think we're supposed to," said Emmett. "It has an official number."

"Nobody has to know," said Lani. "It'd be just for us. It doesn't seem right to send it out without a name, even if it is only a machine."

"I agree," said Dugan.

Bryndis and Sailor were nodding, too.

"What should we name it?" asked Cruz.

"How about Nettie?" offered Bryndis. "Short for Nettles."

Lani grinned. "I like it."

"We have *three* bots," reminded Emmett.

"Stickers," suggested Sailors.

"Nettie, Stickers, and ..." Lani bit her lip.

"Pokey," chimed in Dugan. "You know, because he can both poke you and he pokes along."

It was settled.

Cruz gave his best friend a look. "May I start Nettie *now*?"

She lifted her chin. "You may."

Cruz touched the icon on his screen, and Nettie's mossy base began to creep through the brush. For a few minutes, everyone watched it go, then the members peeled off to help Professor Modi gather firewood, prepare food, and roll out their sleeping bags.

Cruz stayed to make sure everything went smoothly. He held his breath when the plant encountered a bumpy patch of tree roots. The leaves shook as the bot navigated over the ruts and ridges. Cruz didn't exhale until the bot safely made it to the other side. He hoped it would survive. The little plant seemed so small compared to the mammoth forest in front of it. Yet it chugged along, oblivious to the monumental task it had been given.

Cruz watched until he could no longer see the bot's leaves among the tall grasses. "Good luck, Nettie," he whispered. "Hope you find something extraordinary."

"**C**RUZ?"

"Uh-huh?" He was sitting up in the darkness, his tablet propped up on his thighs and his back resting against his inflatable pillow.

Sailor's sleeping bag rustled. "I heard something ... like an animal cry."

"That's my pillow. It has a leak."

"Oh." She chuckled. "What time is it?"

"A quarter to midnight."

"Can't sleep, huh?" Her face appeared from the shadows. She squinted at the light from his screen. "What are you doing?"

"Watching the live feed from Nettie."

She readjusted her own pillow. "Has she seen anything good?"

"Yeah. A bettong, a wombat, and a Tasmanian devil."

"Seriously?" Sailor scooted closer. After a few minutes, she glanced up at him. "No leeches?"

He stiffened. "Not here. You'd have to go west or north into the rainforests," said Cruz, pretending he didn't know what she was referring to.

"I've been meaning to talk to you about that," whispered Sailor. "And to say I'm sorry. I shouldn't have said what I did in Borneo ... I thought you were keeping secrets from me ..."

"It's okay." He could hardly blame her for being right. He *had* been keeping secrets from her. Cruz hated hiding things from his friends. It wasn't fair. The Synthesis knew that he'd been exposed to his mom's serum. Dr. Lu at the Archive knew. Nebula must have known. Why is it everyone knew, except the people that mattered most? "Besides, you were right," Cruz said quietly. "I *was* deliberately trying to get the leech to bite me."

"*What?*"

At her outburst, Bryndis, sleeping on the other side of Sailor, stirred. Sailor froze until Bryndis turned over and settled again. "Why would you do that?" she hissed at Cruz.

"Because my mom's cell-regeneration serum"—spreading his fingers, Cruz placed a hand over his heart—"isn't only engraved in stone."

There! He'd done it. He'd told her. Sort of. He'd kept his deal with the Synthesis. He hadn't divulged what he'd read in his mother's logbook. But would Sailor understand his meaning? Could she read between the lines?

Sailor was slowly pushing herself up. "Crikey," she breathed. "Are you saying—"

"I can't say anything," whispered Cruz.

"I knew you were keeping something from me," said Sailor. "But I didn't realize...I never imagined...How long have you known?"

"Since my trip."

"Can I ask—"

"No. I'm not allowed to talk about it. Not with anybody. Not even Dad or Aunt Marisol."

"Not allowed?" She thought about that for a moment. "That's what you meant at the Terra-Cotta Army museum, wasn't it? That's why you weren't afraid to touch the dragon's blood stone."

He nodded. "There's still a lot I don't understand myself...I have tons of questions, too."

"I'll bet you do."

"Sailor, you can't tell anyone."

"Who would I tell? What would I say? I'm not even sure what I know."

"That makes two of us." Cruz straightened his legs and put his tablet down beside him. He stared up at the clear dark sky, counting the sprinkle of stars flickering through a layer of filmy clouds. "You know what today is?"

"The twenty-second of February."

"It's my mom's birthday."

"It is? No wonder you can't sleep." Sailor looked up, too. It was many minutes before she said softly, "Happy birthday, Cruz's mom."

Snap!

At first, Cruz thought the sound of movement in the brush had come from his tablet, but there was nothing on his screen from Nettie.

"It came from over there." Sailor was looking behind them.

They heard the noise again. This time, closer.

"Should we ... wake Professor Modi?" Sailor gulped.

"We could." He gave her a mischievous grin. "Or we could investigate ourselves."

"I don't know. Every time I explore with you, I end up on the wrong end of a waterfall."

"You're safe this time." Cruz was already wriggling out of his sleeping bag. "There's no waterfall nearby."

"I'm not sure ..."

"Okay." He put on his boots. "Stay, if you want."

She groaned. "I'm coming. Hold on."

"Our MC cameras," he reminded her.

They put on their jackets and dug their cameras out of their packs before carefully stepping over their sleeping teammates. Popping his lens down over his eye to turn on the camera, Cruz began to slowly scan the horizon. He searched the brush for several minutes but didn't see anything. "Whatever it was, it's gone now—"

A hand clamped on to his shoulder. "Straight ahead."

Cruz squared his shoulders and looked through his lens. Was he dreaming?

"Cruz, do you see it?"

He did. He definitely saw it.

"A THYLACINE!" croaked Sailor.

About 15 feet in front of them, a marsupial with thick black stripes along its sleek body ambled across the trail. Its long, stiff tail sloped downward like a kangaroo's, the tip hovering a few inches off the ground. It was, without a doubt, a thylacine! Cruz squinted to see every feature: two round ears, two big eyes, eight longs legs...

Eight legs?

The animal kept moving, and soon something else came into view. Another thylacine—this one much smaller.

Cruz gasped. "A joey!"

In biology, they'd read that a thylacine baby spends the first 12 weeks of its life growing inside its mother's pouch. Cruz knew the joey had to be at least three months old. Still, he seemed so small.

Gangly and awkward, the baby wanted to go a different way, but his mother was having none of it. She came back across the path, nudging him toward the opposite side. Every few steps, mama thylacine would look up at Sailor and Cruz. She did not seem afraid. Just wary. The two animals tipped their heads, as if they were more curious than bothered by the humans gawking at them.

"No one is ever gonna believe us," whispered Cruz.

Pictures! They needed pictures.

Readjusting his tilted MC camera with a shaky hand, Cruz looked through the lens. The pair had made it to the other side of the trail. Mama was already disappearing into the grass. He had to hurry! Cruz thought of the word "photo," then shut his eyes. When he opened them again a few seconds later, the mother and her joey were gone.

"Did you get pics?" Cruz hissed to Sailor.

"Oh no!" She put a hand to her head where her MC camera lens was still pointing straight up. "I got so excited I forgot. You?"

"One. Maybe. I might have blinked too fast. I'll need to see it on my tablet."

"Man, I hope you got something," said Sailor.

They scurried back to camp. Cruz found on his tablet the photo he'd taken only minutes before. The image was perfect. The focus was sharp, the colors true. But there was one problem: The picture did not contain a single thylacine.

Sailor let out a frustrated moan. "We're going be like those wacka-doodles on TV who everyone laughs at—"

"No we're not," said Cruz, "because we aren't going to say anything to anybody about this."

"We aren't?"

"You heard our professors. Scientific evidence is the reason we came, and we're going to have to wait until we get it."

"But that could take . . . forever."

"No it won't," said Cruz, turning off his tablet. "Look, we're deploying a dozen SHOT-bots, between all the explorers. We know there's at least a mom and a joey out there—probably a dad, too. And maybe more. Eventually, one of them is going to walk in front of a bot, right? So until they do, it'll be our . . . secret."

"Great." She yanked off a boot. "Another secret."

"It's the best we can do, Sailor."

She blew out a puff of air. "I know."

Cruz scooted down into his sleeping bag. "We might have to wait before we can tell the rest of the world that thylacines exist, but we know what we saw. And we didn't only see one thylacine, Sailor. We saw two!" Resting his head on his leaky pillow, Cruz turned to look at Sailor. "How many people can say that?"

"Right now? Just you and me."

"The best part is you don't have to eat one of Emmett's stinky socks. Yet."

She laughed. "There's always that."

Cruz searched the cobalt sky until he found the brightest star. *Happy birthday, Mom.*

CRUZ FLUNG HIS DUFFEL to one side of the cabin and his pack to the other, then collapsed headlong onto his bed—his fluffy, warm, bug-free bed.

Home! It had been fun releasing Stickers and Pokey a day after they'd launched Nettie, especially knowing that the thylacines *were* out there. Still, after hiking more than 50 miles through the Tasmanian wilderness, Cruz was eager to get back to *Orion,* to his comfy bed, Chef Kristos's food, and hot water.

"Dibs on the shower," said Emmett.

Darn!

Cruz hopped in after Emmett. Five minutes into his shower, the water turned lukewarm, then cold. All the other explorers must be doing the same thing. When Cruz came out of the bathroom, towel drying his hair, Emmett was on his computers. The emoto-glasses sat on the desk next to him, lifeless ovals.

Cruz tossed his towel over his desk chair. "Do you know what you're going to do about your glasses yet?"

"Uh ... right," said Emmett absently.

"Everything okay?"

"I got a message from Fanchon saying that the results from the Hacker Tracker diagnostic were in. Guess I'm kind of nervous. It doesn't help that it's taking forever to log on to the tech lab's server. It's a slug today."

"What will the test tell you?"

"Pretty much everything: the IP address of the hacker, where the hack originated, when Nebula accessed the glasses, and for how long."

No wonder Emmett was nervous. Cruz dressed and dried his hair. Checking his own tablet, Cruz saw that he had a message from Nyomie telling him that his explorer-adviser conference had been scheduled for the following evening.

It was Sunday afternoon. Ever since they'd lost Taryn, Cruz had always felt a bit blue on Taryn's Fundays. Today, however, he felt none of the usual gloom. Taryn was out there—somewhere. Fanchon said she hadn't erased Taryn's memory or changed her personality. Cruz wondered where she was. Had she been assigned to another Academy ship? More likely, she was still back in Washington, D.C., with Dr. Hightower, getting ready for next year's crop of new recruits. He would never forget standing in line with Sailor that first day at the Academy, as Taryn and Hubbard welcomed him.

Hubbard!

"I'm going to get the pup," Cruz said to his roommate. "Wanna come?"

"Why not?" Emmett sighed. "This is gonna take a while."

A second after Fanchon opened her cabin door, Hubbard catapulted himself into Cruz's open arms. Cruz buried his face in the dog's warm, soft fur and happily inhaled strawberries and bacon.

"Someone is sure glad to see you," said Fanchon. She was holding a leash and Planet Pup. "We were about to go for a walk. I know you just got back, so if you want me to keep him tonight, I don't mind."

"I'll take him." Cruz gave the Westie a good scratching behind the ears. "I've been looking forward to this all day."

Fanchon handed Hubbard's leash and the robotic dog companion to Cruz. She turned to Emmett. "Did you get my note about the Hacker Tracker diagnostic report?"

"Uh-huh. I've been trying to log on to the server but no dice."

"Really? That's strange."

"Maybe it's my computers—"

They felt a slight jolt. The hum of the engines went up slightly in pitch. Cruz knew what that meant. They were leaving. Through Fanchon's porthole, they watched the city of Hobart glide past.

"Quick departure," said Emmett.

"There's a storm coming," explained Fanchon. "Captain Iskandar probably wanted to get out ahead of it."

"Do you know where we're going?" asked Cruz.

"East, I think," said Fanchon. "Not sure we have a destination yet." As the boys turned to go, she said, "Emmett, if you want to stick around for a bit, I can see if I can log in from here to get your Hacker Tracker results."

"Sure." Emmett glanced at Cruz. "Do you mind?"

"Nope," said Cruz. "Hub and I will catch you later."

Fanchon had no sooner shut her door than Hubbard was bouncing on his back feet to try to get the Planet Pup out of Cruz's hands. "You've come a long way, haven't you?" chuckled Cruz. The passage was empty. He didn't see the harm in playing a round or two here.

"Okay, okay, let me turn it on," said Cruz as the dog jumped higher and higher.

He switched on the robotic companion, and almost immediately the ball dropped out of the center of the Saturn-like configuration. Hubbard knew what he wanted to play with, all right! The disk began to spin, then went flying down the corridor, with Hubbard in hot pursuit. Cruz bent to retrieve the ball that Hubbard had left behind. Straightening, he saw Professor Luben's door open at the precise moment the revolving ring reached it.

Uh-oh!

"Professor Luben!" cried Cruz. "Look out!"

His warning came too late.

Cruz's teacher stepped into the hall and was smacked in the chest by the disk. A half second later, he was hit again, this time by one overly excited 20-pound Westie barreling at full speed. Professor Luben flung out an arm to catch the rail along the wall, missed, and went down.

Cruz ran to him. "Are you okay?"

"What do you think?" Professor Luben's face was red. "That dog shouldn't even be here now that—" Letting out a deep breath, he sat up. "Yeah. I'm fine." Taking the hand Cruz offered, he got to his feet. He brushed his hands on his dark pants. "My back's been a bit sore. These last couple of nights on the hard ground..."

"It's my fault," said Cruz. "I shouldn't have turned on Planet Pup here. We usually play in the explorers' passage, where everybody is used to it. I'm sorry." He quickly snapped the leash on to the dog cowering behind him, holding the disk in his mouth. "Come on, Hubbard. Sorry again, Professor Luben."

"No harm done," said his teacher, though his grimace did not disappear.

Cruz and Hubbard quickly trotted down the passage and through the atrium. They didn't slow down until they were on home turf: the explorers' passage. Only then did Cruz exhale. He hoped he wouldn't get in trouble, but that look on his teacher's face...

And with his evaluation a day away!

"I'll probably get a talking-to from Nyomie," Cruz said to Hub as they headed out to the stern deck. Once the Westie had finished his business, Cruz took him back to cabin 202 to play. It wasn't as much space as Hubbard preferred, but it was the best he could do for now. "I'll reserve us some time in the CAVE next weekend," Cruz promised as the Westie romped around his bed. "We'll use the Rock Creek Park program. You'll really be able to run there."

"Fanchon to Cruz Coronado." The tech lab chief's voice crackled through Cruz's comm pin. She sounded far away.

"Cruz, here."

"Please report to the tech lab right away."

"Uh . . . sure. Is Emmett with you? Is everything all right?"

No answer.

"Let's go, Hub," said Cruz, attaching the dog's leash. "We'll get your walk in . . . or maybe your run."

They jogged most of the way to the lab. Inside, Cruz and Hubbard waited for the tech lab chief or her assistant to appear from the labyrinth of cubicles as usual. They hung out for several minutes, but nobody showed up. Weird.

"Fanchon? Dr. Vanderwick?" Cruz asked into his comm pin. He glanced down at Hubbard. "I guess she must have gotten busy."

The dog lifted an ear.

Cruz wasn't sure what to do. Should he go, or wait a little longer? Fanchon had sounded pretty serious. He didn't want to leave yet. He pressed his comm pin. "Cruz to—"

"Help."

The feeble cry had come from somewhere in the lab.

Overhead, the green lights flickered. Half of them went out.

"Fanchon?" called Cruz.

Silence.

"Come on, Hub." Cruz wrapped the end of Hubbard's leash around his wrist and hurried into the cubicles with the Westie at his side. Which way should he go? He jogged left, then right, his eyes searching for a colorful head scarf and apron and pink shoes. He dashed left, then right, poking his head into every workspace as he called her name. "Fanchon?"

Cruz pulled up. They were through the maze. He'd reached the end of the compartment. Fanchon wasn't here. The lights above the cabinets next to him dimmed, then shut off. What was going on? A power surge? A blown circuit?

"*Ruff!*" It was short and sharp—Hubbard's warning bark. The dog retreated a couple of steps back into the aisle between the cubicles.

"I know what you mean, Hub," whispered Cruz. "I don't like it either."

Cruz felt something cold snake around his neck.

"Don't move," a digitized voice said into his left ear as icy fingers clamped on to him. "Or it'll be the last thing you *both* do."

21

IT WASN'T the first time Cruz had heard the scratchy, emotionless voice. It belonged to the Nebula agent who'd attacked him at *Orion*'s Halloween party. He or she had mysteriously disappeared after the incident, but Cruz had a feeling he hadn't seen the last of the assailant in the red-jeweled mask.

"Arms down, flat against your sides, explorer," came the order from behind him. "You wouldn't want Hubbard to get hurt because you couldn't follow directions."

Cruz obeyed. He was unable to reach the octopod, his comm pin, or Mell's remote now—and his foe knew it. Cruz felt a tug on the lanyard he wore. The cipher was sliding up his chest. He licked dry lips. "You're Zebra, aren't you?"

"You've heard about me."

Cruz felt the cipher tumble over the top of his tee. A hand came around the side of Cruz's arm. It reached across his chest.

Hubbard let out a low growl.

"It's all right, Hub." Keeping his arms tight against his sides, Cruz stretched out his fingers to pet the dog's head. "Everything's going to be okay."

If Cruz had been alone, he might have tried to fight Zebra, but with Hubbard next to him? No way. Cruz took a deep breath to steady his fluttering heart. Then another. What was the agent doing? He seemed to be taking a long time to get the stones over his head.

Get on with it already!

Cruz dropped his chin. The circle of marble was now hanging outside of his shirt, over his heart. Yet, Zebra *still* didn't have it. The agent was trying to grab the cipher but couldn't. Each time Cruz's fingers tried to latch on to the stones, they slid away. "What have you done?" demanded the computerized voice. "Why can't I touch it? Why won't it come off?"

"I...I don't know," stammered Cruz. "I'm n-not doing anything."

"Woof!" Hubbard was trying to get between them. He must have heard the panic in Cruz's voice. *"Woof! WOOF!"*

"I have a fire lance," said Zebra. "Make him stop or I'll—"

"Don't!" cried Cruz. He didn't know what a fire lance was, but it didn't sound like anything he wanted to mess with. "I'll make him stop, but I need to move. I'm going to kneel, let him off his leash, and send him to the other side of the lab, okay? He's got a toy basket over by Fanchon's desk. That should keep him busy."

"Do it."

Cruz went down on one knee. He turned his shoulders slightly, hoping to see something that might give him a clue as to the agent's identity.

"Easy, buddy." Cruz reached for the hook on Hubbard's leash. Out of the corner of his eye, he took in what the spy was wearing: black pants, black socks, and black shoes. He couldn't help the tiny gasp that escaped his lips. It was the shoes that gave Zebra away.

Red roses. The shoes were printed with red roses.

Dr. Vanderwick! She was Zebra!

Really? *She* was Zebra?

Cruz would never have suspected Fanchon's assistant of working for Nebula! Yet, it made sense in a weird way. Dr. Vanderwick had access to every piece of technology the explorers used and every system on the ship. There was nothing she couldn't monitor, tweak, sabotage, or destroy.

"Grrrrr!" Hubbard was baring his teeth at the agent.

"Hurry up!" Dr. Vanderwick was prodding Cruz between the shoulder blades with something sharp.

Unclipping the leash, Cruz shooed the dog back into the cubicles. "Go to your basket. Go and stay there, Hub," he ordered.

The Westie hesitated.

"Go!" shouted Cruz, his harsh tone surprising even himself.

Hubbard whimpered. Seeing those sad, confused button eyes, an ache pierced Cruz's heart. He wished he could explain to the dog that it was for his own good.

Hanging his head, Hubbard scampered away.

"Stand up," ordered the digitized voice.

Cruz obeyed, slowly straightening. His back was still to her. Next to his shoulder appeared the end of a metal poker, its rounded tip glowing scarlet. The fire lance? Suddenly, a jawbreaker-size orb of flames shot out! Cruz ducked as the fireball whizzed past his ear. It hit the metal door of the merry-go-lab, breaking up in a shower of sparks.

"Whoa!" Cruz put a hand to his temple to see if he'd been singed. "Are you nuts, Dr. Vanderwick?"

Cruz instantly regretted his words. It was a dumb mistake. If he'd let her have the cipher without revealing he knew who she was, the assistant tech lab chief *might* have released him. But now she couldn't let him go. And they both knew it.

Cruz turned to face Dr. Vanderwick. Still holding the fire lance, she used her other hand to rip off the red-jeweled mask that had disguised her voice and identity. Her face was pink, shiny with sweat, and her usually neat bun had come undone. Several loose strands of hair clung to her cheeks.

There could be no doubt now: Dr. Vanderwick was Zebra.

One side of her mouth went up. "You don't seem all that surprised."

"I . . . I am surprised," stammered Cruz. His attention was drawn away for a moment by the top of a peach balloon in the cubicle behind her. Funny. He didn't remember seeing it when he came in. "I didn't think you'd ever do . . . I mean, you did some pretty awful things."

"Not awful." She let the mask fall to the floor. "Necessary."

Cruz was going over the list in his head. "You trapped us in a storage closet at the Academy and pumped in toxic gas."

"Guilty."

"You ransacked our cabin and spied on us through the security cams and Emmett's glasses."

"True." There was no remorse in her tone.

"And sabotaged the UCC helmet."

"One of my best efforts, though not good enough, sadly."

"The merry-go-lab . . . and Aunt Marisol's flower . . ." That was one good thing: Aunt Marisol was not the Nebula agent, as Cruz had feared—a fact he would celebrate if he got out of this alive.

"Fanchon and you were both getting too close. I saw an opportunity and took it. Spur-of-the-moment move to throw you off my trail." Still holding him at bay with the fire lance, she reached for her tablet. "You forgot the poison in your duffel bag."

No, he had not forgotten.

Cruz felt a muscle in his jaw twitch. "You could have killed Bryndis."

"Me? You're as much to blame as I am for that one. Next time, use your own duffel bag. Can I help it if she was in the wrong place at the wrong time?"

Cruz stiffened. He hated that saying. And how coldly she'd said it. The balloon behind Dr. Vanderwick was swaying back and forth, likely caught in the lab's air-conditioning stream.

The journal! Cruz had nearly asked Dr. Vanderwick to help him fix his mom's journal. What a disaster that would have been! Cruz felt his temper begin to simmer. "You're supposed to look out for us," he cried. "We all trusted you—me, Fanchon, Dr. Hightower, the Academy—"

"*The Academy?*" She spit the words, as if they tasted sour. "I have no loyalty to the Academy. Not anymore. Do you know what it's like to never get the credit you're due? Of course you don't. I work as hard as Fanchon, often harder, but does anybody notice? No, you're all too busy gushing over *her.*" Dark gray eyes blazed. "Twenty-two years I've worked for the Academy, watching other scientists pass me by, waiting for the day I would get to be tech chief on a ship of my own. Did I say anything? Complain? Make demands? No! I took it. I took every bit because I thought *my* loyalty would be rewarded, that one day my chance would come. But it never did."

"I'm sure Dr. Hightower—"

"Dr. Hightower and the Academy abandoned me. Only Nebula saw what I had to offer. It finally gave me what I deserved—"

"Money," retorted Cruz.

"*Money?* Haven't you been listening?" Her cheeks flamed red. "You think that's what motivates me? I do what I do because I have a passion for science. Nebula invested in me—my research and my *ideas.*"

Cruz narrowed his eyes at her. "Now you're helping them steal someone else's ideas."

"Your mother was the one that betrayed Nebula," snarled Dr. Vanderwick. "Without their money, Petra would never have been able to develop the serum. But when she found out she could make bigger bucks selling it to another company, she refused to turn over the formula."

"That's not true! My mom told me what happened—"

"Believe what you choose." The assistant tech lab chief grunted. "We all do, in the end. I don't have all day. Give me the stone, Cruz, or—"

"You'll kill me?" he challenged. "Are you sure? I mean, you don't have a UCC helmet or a duffel bag to do it for you this time."

"I have everything I need right here." The fire lance shook in her hand.

The orange balloon that had been floating behind Dr. Vanderwick was rising from the cubicle. Cruz tried to ignore it, but it had broken free of its tether. Must be a pretty strong breeze from the vent, thought Cruz. As the balloon drifted upward, he expected to see it tied off at the bottom with a ribbon or string tail, but there was no bottom. No tail. As the rubbery peach globe began to turn the color of a sunset, Cruz realized what was going on. This was no balloon. It was Fanchon's sensotivia gel!

"Uh … Dr. Vanderwick?" Cruz watched the gel begin to change shape. It was separating into two halves, like the weird blobby goo in a lava lamp. He pointed to it. "I think you'd … uh … better look—"

"Yeah. Right. Give me the stone!"

As the gel oozed over the partition, Cruz remembered how he'd upset it once before. To help settle the temperamental material, he tried to bring to mind things that made him happy. Hubbard. Macadamia-nut ice cream. Surfing. His dad. Aunt Marisol. Bryndis. But none of his joyful thoughts were working. Instead, the ball was growing larger and turning deeper orange. "Um … Dr. Vanderwick?" Cruz put up his hands. "Maybe we should calm down and talk about what's bothering you—"

"*I will not calm down!*"

Like two bear paws, the sensotivia gel stretched for her.

Dr. Vanderwick lifted the fire lance. "CRUZ, GIVE ME THE—Arggggh!"

Wrapping its gooey claws around her neck, the sensotivia gel began to cover Dr. Vanderwick. The sludge rolled over her shoulders, arms, and hands, moving to her waist and hips, then—finally—legs, ankles, and feet. It took less than 10 seconds for the wave to blanket her in goo a foot thick. Only her head remained free.

Stepping back, Cruz let out a sigh. *That should hold her!*

He saw flecks of orange splatter against the walls of the compartment. Suddenly, a ball of flames was soaring toward him. Dr. Vanderwick had shot the fire lance through the sensotivia gel! Cruz dropped to the floor, and the fiery orb hit the corner of the wall. In a matter of seconds, the blaze spread. The cabinets were on fire!

Scrambling to his feet, Cruz rushed for the extinguisher attached to the far wall. He pulled the pin, aimed the nozzle at the flame, and squeezed the trigger. A burst of white foam spewed from the cone. It took only a minute or so to put out the fire, though it felt like hours. Coughing, Cruz waved the smoke away. He was relieved that the sprinklers hadn't gone off. Did water dissolve sensotivia gel or only make it angrier? He had no idea and really didn't want to find out.

While he was busy battling the blaze, the sensotivia gel had quickly reclaimed Dr. Vanderwick. Able to move her hands slightly, the assistant tech lab chief tried to shoot the fire lance again. Nothing happened. The gel must be jamming it. Dr. Vanderwick still held her tablet in her other hand, although Cruz had a feeling that if she let go of her computer, it would remain suspended within the same blob that held her fast. Thrashing her head from side to side, she tried to wriggle free, but it was no use.

Cruz dropped the empty extinguisher.

It was over.

His legs felt like spaghetti. His arms, too. He wasn't sure he could even summon the strength to hit his comm pin and call for help.

"Hey, Fanchon? Should Hubbard be running around here—" Nyomie came around a corner of a cubicle. The Westie was with her. "Oh my!" One look at Dr. Vanderwick, and she let out a laugh. "What happened here?"

"Cruz attacked me with the sensotivia gel," cried Dr. Vanderwick.

Cruz safely tucked the cipher back into his shirt. "That's ... not true ..." he huffed.

"You aren't going to believe *him,* are you?" The lab assistant craned her neck. "I'm trapped in this ... this goop. Look at me! Just look at me!"

"I'm ... uh ... looking, all right." Nyomie cocked an uncertain eyebrow. "Cruz, I didn't take you for one to pull these kinds of pranks."

He shook his head. "I ... I ..."

"And, Sidril," she went on, "you do kind of remind me of the gelatin fruit salad my mom makes at Thanksgiving. Although she floats pineapple in hers—"

"Just get me out of here!" shrieked Dr. Vanderwick.

"Don't do it, Nyomie," warned Cruz. "This was no prank. *She* is dangerous."

Seeing his face, Nyomie's grin faded. She took a cautious step back. "I think I'll let security sort this one out."

Cruz relaxed. The more people they got in here, the better.

His adviser tapped her comm pin. "Nyomie Byron to security."

Bending to beg Hubbard's forgiveness, Cruz tapped his own comm pin. "Cruz Coronado to Marisol Coronado."

"They won't answer you," shot Dr. Vanderwick. "No one will. I've shut off all communications coming into and going out of the lab."

"You did *what*?" Nyomie glanced from Cruz to the scientist encased in orange gel. "Okay, Sidril, what's really going on here?"

"You were wrong about me, Cruz," snarled Dr. Vanderwick. "I'm not afraid to take action. I have my instructions from Nebula: Destroy the cipher. If that means taking the ship down with it, well, I'm prepared to do that." She tilted her head down, her chin dipping into the goo. Dr. Vanderwick pressed a key on her tablet.

What was she doing? Cruz ran closer to peer through the thick gelatin. On her screen was a diagram of the UCC helmet. Beneath it, red numbers were counting down.

4:59 ... 4:58 ... 4:57 ...

"What is that?" demanded Cruz.

"If I were you, I'd stop talking and start running," clipped Dr. Vanderwick. "Not that there's anywhere to run. You've got less than five minutes."

"Until what?" he rasped.

"What else?" Her lips twisted into a smirk. "Until Fanchon's precious UCC helmet self-destructs."

22

CRUZ SPUN to Nyomie. "I'll get to the passage, call the bridge, and tell them to sound the alarm to abandon—"

"No," she broke in. "You'll only send a panic through the ship. We'd never get everyone off in time. We've got to stop this ourselves."

"Our . . . selves?" Was she kidding? "H-how are we supposed to do that?"

"First things first." Closing her eyes and scrunching her nose, Nyomie plunged an arm into the sensotivia gel enveloping the tech lab chief. She latched on to Dr. Vanderwick's tablet and began sliding it toward her. The scientist fought to hold on to her device, even as the gel began creeping up the back of her head. Cruz latched on to his adviser's arm and helped pull. Inch by inch, they eased the tablet through the goo. "Almost . . . there . . ." Nyomie gritted her teeth. "One more . . . tug . . . Got it!"

Cruz grabbed a nearby towel, and Nyomie quickly wiped the screen clean.

"You won't be able to defuse it," taunted Dr. Vanderwick, lifting her chin to keep it above the still-creeping gel. "Not even Fanchon could shut it off."

"We'll see about that." Nyomie began typing on the tablet.

"It's not a big helmet," said Cruz. "How much damage could it—"

"Plenty!" bit Dr. Vanderwick. "I used a new liquid compound I've been working on. A few drops did the trick. Once the detonator triggers, it'll blow a hole in the ship big enough to sink her. You're wasting your time, Nyomie. You'll never find it."

"Don't be so sure." Nyomie's fingers were flying over the keys so fast they were a blur.

Cruz had an idea. "Nyomie, have you ever played twenty questions?"

"What?"

"Twenty questions, you know, the game?"

"A game? You want to play a game *now*?"

"Sort of." Cruz dug out the virtugraph. He crossed his arms in front of him, tucking the compass behind his left elbow. He pressed the sleeping dove and aimed the instrument at Dr. Vanderwick. "Nyomie, I bet the UCC is on the bridge," he said.

"That's where it is, all right," cackled Dr. Vanderwick.

The black needle swung to point toward the scientist. "It's not there," Cruz whispered to Nyomie. "Your turn. Make a guess. Do it so she hears you."

His adviser paused long enough to glance at the virtugraph. "What is that?"

"A Fanchon original. Hurry. Ask. Loudly."

"Uh ... it must be in the library," called Nyomie.

"Yep, that's where I put it," said Dr. Vanderwick. "It's shelved under *K* for 'KABOOM'!" She let out a crazy laugh that sent a shiver through Cruz.

Again, the black arrow.

"The CAVE?" tried Cruz.

"I considered that ... I really did," said Dr. Vanderwick very seriously. "But no. Monsieur Legrand is quite clever. I couldn't risk it."

Cruz watched the red needle swing around. True statement.

He kept quizzing her, listing the galley, the dining room, the ship's store, the observation deck, sick bay, aquatics, the laundry room, and the faculty and explorers' passages. However, the helmet wasn't in any of those places. And they were running out of time. The countdown clock on Dr. Vanderwick's tablet had reached the three-minute mark.

A droplet of sweat rolled off Cruz's nose, splashing onto the face of the compass. "It's here ... in the tech lab," he said, his voice shaky. He didn't really believe that, but he didn't know where else to try.

Dr. Vanderwick rolled her eyes. "I'd have to be pretty stupid to do something under Fanchon's nose, wouldn't I?"

The needle spun. The black arrow was pointing to the gel. She was lying!

"It *is* here!" Cruz hissed to Nyomie, then to Dr. Vanderwick he yelled, "I think it's in the merry-go-lab."

"Ick!" Dr. Vanderwick spit out a mouthful of gel. "Nice try ... but wrong."

The black arrow didn't budge. The merry-go-lab had three compartments.

"In the storage room?" asked Cruz.

"Nope."

The red arrow swiveled her way. Truth.

"You're wasting time," sang Dr. Vanderwick. "You've got less than two minutes. Is this how you really want to spend it?"

"It's in the robotics lab," pressed Cruz.

"Nope. Try again. I am so enjoying our little game."

The black arrow swapped places with the red. Another lie!

"That's it, Nyomie!" cried Cruz. "It's in the robotics room of the merry-go-lab."

"Let's go!" They bolted for the door.

"You'll never ... get in," coughed Dr. Vanderwick.

She was right. "We don't have access," said Cruz.

Nyomie's fingers hit the keypad: 4-2-9-2-4-4. She put her eye to the iris scanner.

He gasped. "How did you—"

The door opened.

Nyomie thrust Dr. Vanderwick's sticky tablet into his hands. "Stay here."

Cruz glanced down.

1:47 ... 1:46 ... 1:45 ...

"You'll never make it." Dr. Vanderwick read his mind.

His heart booming, Cruz rushed into the merry-go-lab. Nyomie had thrown open the doors of one of the bottom cabinets and was pawing through the contents. Crawling into the cabinet, she pulled out the UCC helmet.

Cruz shook his head. "That was fast!"

"I heard the ticking." She was inspecting the helmet.

"You must have good ears 'cause I didn't—"

"Get me a flathead screwdriver!" she ordered. "Second drawer from the end."

Cruz obeyed. Nyomie unscrewed the top section of the helmet and gently removed it from the base. She peered inside. "Uh-oh."

"Uh-oh? What-oh? You always cut the green wire." Cruz gulped. "It's usually the green one, right? Unless that's the one that detonates it. It could be the blue wire, but it's never the red wire. Whatever you do, do *not* cut the red wire." Cruz could hear himself babbling but couldn't seem to stop.

"Cruz! How much time?"

"Um . . . one minute. What are you gonna do, cut *all* the wires?"

Two saucer eyes looked at him. "No wires."

"No wires?"

"She's right. We can't stop the self-destruct sequence."

"Now what?"

Nyomie put her hands around the base of the helmet. She picked it up. "Get out of the way."

"Huh?"

"Move!"

Cruz jumped back. His adviser charged out of the merry-go-lab with him on her heels.

"Too late!" choked Dr. Vanderwick. "Too . . . late!" The sensotivia gel, now a fiery red, covered most of her head. It was closing in around her face, moving over her chin and cheeks.

"Hubbard, come on!" called Cruz. Ahead of him, Nyomie was already weaving through the cubicles.

Cruz ran after his adviser. He did not look back. Nyomie dodged right and left, zigzagging through the partitions. "Get the door!" she cried, moving to her right to allow Cruz to pass.

Cruz opened the tech lab door. Nyomie shot through it and made a left turn. Cruz hurried to catch to her in the passage. Side by side, with Hubbard on their heels, they raced past the galley, dining room, classrooms, and faculty offices. He knew where she was headed.

Pouring it on, Cruz got out in front and yanked open the door to the stern deck. The outdoor deck was empty, thank goodness. Nyomie made a beeline for the back rail.

"Ten seconds," said Cruz. "Throw it!"

"Get down!" she shouted.

Cruz dropped to his knees on the deck. "Hubbard!" He pulled the dog in under his body.

Nine . . . eight . . . seven . . .

Nyomie was still holding the helmet. What was she waiting for?

Why didn't she toss it overboard?

Five … four … three …

Like an Olympic athlete throwing a shot put, she spun once before hurling the helmet into the air. It soared upward over the stern, a spinning black orb. Nyomie dropped to the deck beside him. Cruz felt an arm lock over his back.

BOOM!

The helmet exploded mere seconds before it would have splashed into the sea. Tucking his head, Cruz curled himself around Hubbard to protect the dog from the bits of shrapnel pelting them. He felt a wave of heat as the shock rocked the ship. Cruz and Nyomie clung to each other. Only when the swaying stopped did they dare lift their heads.

"You okay?" asked Nyomie, not releasing him.

"Yeah. You?"

"Uh-huh."

Huddled against Cruz's stomach, Hubbard was trembling, but he was all right.

"I realize this might not be the best time to ask..." said Cruz, his heart still hammering against his ribs. "But I need to know."

"What?" She panted, brushing hair from her eyes.

"You knew the key code to get into robotics and where to find the screwdriver... How?"

Nyomie's mouth dropped. "Oh, did I? I... I... didn't realize... You know how it is when you're not thinking about things... Just lucky, I guess."

"No, it was more than that. It was like you'd been there before." Cruz looked into Nyomie's brown eyes. Searching. Begging. Hoping. "Please... I have to know the truth. I *have* to. Are you...?"

Arms tightened around him. "Yes, Cruz." Her voice was the faintest whisper. "It's me."

"**T**HAT'S WHY I COULDN'T LOG** in to the Hacker Tracker database," said Emmett. "Dr. Vanderwick was blocking me. She knew the results from my emoto-glasses diagnostics would lead us to the IP address of her tablet, even though she'd done her best to hide it by using a virtual private network."

"We figure she'd tried to tamper with the results but couldn't,"

Cruz explained to Lani and Sailor, who were sitting side by side on his bed. "Naturally, the software Fanchon had written was hacker-proof. Zebra was stuck." He took a seat on the floor next to Hubbard's bed. "The best she could do was stall Emmett, but she knew it was only a matter of time before Fanchon and he discovered the truth. She had to act. Getting me up to the lab was her last chance to grab the cipher and finish me off." Cruz stroked Hubbard's head. "Of course, she didn't count on the sensotivia gel."

Sailor let out a low whistle. "I guess it really is true. Hate destroys the hater."

"The gel won't be destroying anything anymore," said Emmett. "Fanchon feels it's too dangerous to have aboard. She's sealing it in a hazmat container and sending it back to the Society's main lab in Washington, D.C."

Cruz couldn't help wondering if the gel would end up in the Archive.

With the whole ship buzzing about the explosion, everyone had been told that an experiment in the tech lab had gone wrong. Fortunately, no one but Cruz had seen the UCC helmet in flight, so it was assumed that Nyomie was disposing of the dangerous invention that had taken Dr. Vanderwick's life.

"Poor Fanchon," sighed Sailor. "To find out that your assistant, someone you worked with and considered a friend, was spying for Nebula and sabotaging your work ..."

"And then to lose the UCC helmet," added Lani.

"If I know Fanchon, she'll build another one—a better one," said Emmett.

They all nodded.

"There's still something I don't get," said Lani. "Cruz, you said Dr. Vanderwick tried to steal the cipher from around your neck when you were in the lab but couldn't do it. Why not?"

"Oh, that." Grinning, Cruz lifted the lanyard from his neck. He held it out, the circle of seven interconnecting stones dangling in front of Lani. "Take it."

Lani raised her eyebrows but did as he asked. Reaching for the black marble, her fingers were stopped an inch shy of the stones. "A force field!"

"Not just any force field," said Cruz, easily taking the cipher with his other hand. "A *bio* force field. It's synced up to my bioelectromagnetic signature, you know, the electrical impulses sent out by my brain, heart, nerves, and muscles. Basically, as long as the stone remains on my body, I'm the only one who can touch it."

"Cracker!" Sailor looked from Cruz to Emmett. "When did you guys do this?"

"*We* didn't," said Cruz, slipping the lanyard back over his head.

"Fanchon!" said the girls in unison.

"It's Fanchon's Bio-Net Level Four force field," explained Emmett. "I ran it through a couple of tests. No question about it. We're not exactly sure when she set it up. It could have been weeks ago."

Lani put a hand to her mouth. "Then she must know about your mom's formula, the cipher—everything!"

Cruz bit his lip. "I haven't had the chance to talk to her about it, but…"

"How long do you think—"

"Since I first came on board *Orion*," said Cruz. "She tried to tell me in a dozen different ways—even made the octopod for me—but I wasn't ready to trust her."

"I'm just glad Zebra is finally out of the picture," said Emmett. "One spy down, one to go."

"Speaking of one to go," jumped in Sailor. "When do we open the journal for the last clue?"

"We'll have to wait until tomorrow," answered Cruz. "T—Nyomie wants to take tomorrow off, so she moved my evaluation up to tonight. I have to leave at seven."

Lani looked at her wrist. "Uh … it's five after seven now."

"Gotta go." Cruz dropped a kiss on Hubbard's head on his way out.

Scurrying down the passage, Cruz zipped through his adviser's open door.

Nyomie gave him a hug. "You're seven minutes late."

Cruz laughed. She was sounding more and more like Taryn all the time. Cruz chose the comfy cream-colored wingback, because he knew the red floral was her favorite.

"Are you all right?" asked Taryn, closing the door behind him. "That was pretty intense today."

"I'm okay." Other than a small cut on the back of his arm, which was already healing, he was fine. "How about you, Taryn?"

"Cruz, you can't do that. You can't call me Taryn."

"Sorry. I ... forgot."

"You can't forget. I'm Nyomie. You can't slip up. Not once. Not ever."

"I won't." Cruz twisted a loose string on the arm of his chair, wrapping it around his finger. "Could you ... tell me what it stands for?"

"What?"

"Your name. Fanchon told me Secliff stood for Sentient Emotive Cybernetic Life-Form. I couldn't help wondering what Nyomie Byron stood for—"

"Nothing."

"Nothing?"

"That's right. This time, Fanchon let me choose my own name. I borrowed Byron from Ada Byron Lovelace, the first person credited for writing instructions for a computer program. Funny, though. I also read she didn't think much of the possibility of artificial intelligence. Of course, it *was* the 1800s. I like to think she'd reconsider her position if she were alive today ... and met me."

"And Nyomie?"

"Fanchon's mother's name."

"Nice."

"Cruz, you have to promise—"

"I won't say a word. I'm good at keeping secrets."

"That you are." Nyomie slid her tablet onto her lap. "Let's start your conference. Let's see ... your OS band shows you're in good health. Heart rate and blood pressure are fine. You're sleeping and eating well and getting plenty of activity. Oh, you've grown two-point-four inches since you came to the Academy."

Cruz stuck out his legs to show her his ankles. "I could use some new pants."

"I'll take care of that. What else …? Ah, your grades are excellent. You're making all A's and your professors have glowing things to say about you, although a couple of them have commented that you've missed class on occasion. I see you are making regular calls home to your dad. Good. I've had the chance to talk to your aunt and your father, and both indicate that you are adjusting well to the travel and say that, overall, you love being an explorer."

"I do," he said. "More than anything."

"That's good to hear, especially after all you've been through. I know your mom was an explorer, too. And a top one. Do you feel like you have to live up to her … legacy?"

He didn't want to lie. "Maybe a little."

"It's hard, filling someone else's shoes." She leaned forward. "Here's my last and final word to the wise: Don't even try. Just be yourself, Cruz Coronado. Your mom would want that. We all want that."

Cruz grinned.

"Now, is there anything *you* want to talk about?" asked Nyomie.

Cruz rested his elbow on the arm rest. "There is *one* thing …"

"Go ahead." She settled back into her chair and crossed her legs. "You are my only session this evening, so we can take as much time as you need to discuss whatever is on your mind—issues, gripes, friends, school, gear, dreams, goals—you name it. I'm here for you."

"This is more of a friend thing," said Cruz.

"Not a problem. As you know, all adviser-explorer conversations are kept strictly confidential."

"It *is* about someone you know," explained Cruz. "He's furry and white, and he's missed you almost more than anyone around here."

"Ahh!" She chuckled. "I've missed him, too. So very much." Her voice broke with emotion. "Thank you for taking good care of Hubbard while I was . . . away. I knew you would."

"I tried to finish crocheting the sweater you started for him, you know, the one in Firefly Summer yarn?" He grimaced. "Crocheting is harder than it looks."

"I could teach you."

"That's okay." He waved her off. "I'm much better with Planet Pup. Hub and I play with it almost every night. Usually about now."

"Really?" Nyomie set her tablet aside. "I think we're done here, explorer, don't you?"

"Definitely." Cruz sprung from his chair. "I'll get Hubbard and Planet Pup and be right back. Don't go anywhere, okay?"

"Not a chance."

23

"NO...NO!"

Hearing the cries, Cruz stopped in the passage. It was Monday after-noon, a half hour after classes let out, and he was on his way to see his aunt. They'd had little time to talk since the events of the day before.

"But how can that be?" It was Ali. "I was going to name it. Professor Ishikawa said I got to name it!"

Less than five feet from the door to Aunt Marisol's office, Cruz halted. He took a few steps back.

"Professor Ishikawa, Dr. Holland, Dr. Hightower, and I are all terribly sorry," Aunt Marisol was saying. "The Academy's database should have been updated, and we take full responsibility for that. This is also why it's important to always verify our discoveries."

"I don't believe you," snapped Ali.

"If you'd like to see Dr. Banicki's letter ... He's an experienced lepidopterist, and he assures us that this moth is known and has been classified—"

"I know what's going on. You did this on purpose. You're trying to help Cruz win the North Star award."

Cruz's breath stuck in his windpipe.

"Ali, that's not true," said Aunt Marisol. "I would never—"

"I'm calling my mom and dad!"

Frantically searching for a place to hide, Cruz ducked into the closest open door. It happened to lead into the conference room. Cruz plastered himself to the wall next to the door. A moment later, Ali marched past, his hands balled into fists. Only after he no longer heard angry footsteps did Cruz stick his head out. Seeing no one in the corridor, he tiptoed into his aunt's office.

Aunt Marisol was standing at the tiny porthole, staring blankly at the choppy waves. She'd wrapped her arms around herself, though it wasn't cold in her small office. "You heard?"

"Ali's moth, huh?"

"Not anymore, it isn't."

"He was kind of brutal ... the way he talked to you ... accused you."

"It's all right." She sighed. "He was upset. I know once he's had time to calm down, he'll accept the situation with the same courage and poise we've come to expect of all of our explorers."

Cruz hoped so. The guy could sure hold a grudge. "Aunt Marisol, do you think that Ali could be Jaguar? I mean, he's so mad all the time."

She sucked in her lower lip. "My gut says no. It's not the angry ones you have to worry about. They push you away and keep you at a distance. A spy doesn't do that. A spy wants to get close, wants to be your friend. That's the person you have to worry about. A friend."

Danger is closer than you know.

Taking his hand from his pocket, Cruz stretched out his arm. "I think this is yours."

"What is— Where did you find that?" She grinned when she saw the little white daisy with the yellow jewel.

"The tech lab."

"The tech lab?" Her eyes narrowed as she tried to recall how she could have lost it there.

"Dr. Vanderwick took it ... or found it," he said. "She dropped it next to the door to the merry-go-lab to make me think you'd sabotaged the lab when Fanchon and I were inside."

"Oh, goodness..."

"She wanted me to think you were Zebra." Cruz shifted from one foot to the other. "And ... for a minute there, I did. But only for a minute, Aunt Marisol."

She stared at the flower. "I see."

"Are you ... mad?"

"Mad?" She lifted her head, tears glazing her brown eyes. In three steps, she was across the little office and her arms were around him. "Mad is the last thing I am, Cruz Sebastian. To think of what that woman could have done to you—to all of us."

Cruz hugged back just as tightly.

After a while, his aunt let him go. "I talked to Dr. Hightower last night. Naturally, she was pretty upset. She was glad to hear that everyone was all right and that the ship suffered no damage. She did have one question, however, that I couldn't answer."

Cruz glanced up. "What was that?"

"She wanted to know how you so quickly and correctly guessed that Sidril had placed the rigged helmet in the merry-go-lab."

"I'm not supposed to tell you," he said. "But I will. Don't tell Fanchon." Cruz showed her the virtugraph and explained how he'd used it to narrow down the location of the helmet. "Pretty cool, huh?"

"Uh ... yeah. That was genius." Still, a shadow crossed his aunt's face.

"Something wrong?"

"It's an incredible invention and kind of Fanchon to let you test it, Cruz, but be careful, okay?"

"What do you mean?" He'd already been thinking about how to use the virtugraph to help him root out Jaguar. He couldn't pose an obvious question to another explorer, of course, but what if he asked things in a roundabout way? He could say something like "My dad is thinking of applying for a job at Nebula. Do you know anyone who works there?" Cruz figured a few questions like that could whittle down the list of suspects pretty quickly.

"Things aren't always black and white, or in this case black and red," said his aunt. "Sometimes, they're gray."

"I get it," said Cruz. "You're saying some people have a good reason for lying or a bad reason for telling the truth."

"Yes, but it's more than that. The virtugraph can take into account physical and behavioral characteristics, but it can't factor in all the other things that motivate people, like relationships, circumstances, or intentions."

"That's why I like it," insisted Cruz. "It measures all the things I can't. Just like our OS bands. Besides, I thought we were supposed to be learning to use technology."

"Use it, yes. Depend on it, no."

His shoulders sagged. "You don't like the compass."

"I didn't say that." She sighed. "A compass may point you in the right direction, which is all well and good, but it can't take you where you want to go. You have to do that on your own."

"Huh?"

"All I'm saying is utilize it for the tool that it is but rely on your own judgment. Trust your instincts. View the whole picture. Then make up your mind. Okay?"

"Okay, Aunt Marisol." Cruz was still a bit confused. He put the virtugraph back into his pocket.

"I have a lot of work to catch up on." She slid in behind her desk. "See you at dinner?"

"Sure." Walking out of her office, Cruz couldn't help feeling as if his aunt had been trying to tell him something important, and that whatever it was had nothing to do with the truth compass.

But what?

"CRUZ, I THINK YOU'D BETTER take a look at this." Emmett turned from his computers.

"One sec." Cruz was pouring chunks of beef and gravy into Hubbard's bowl. Setting the bowl down on the mat in front of the dog, Cruz went to peer over his roommate's shoulder. He saw a freeze-frame of a forest at night. "Is that—"

"Nettie," said Emmett. "Ever since we launched our SHOT-bots, I've been logging in whenever I can to view the stream and recordings."

"Oh my gosh, Emmett! Are you saying...? Did Nettie find a...a...?"

"Thylacine? No." He pushed the earthworm glasses up his nose. "But I did see something else that surprised me almost as much." He nodded to the screen. "This is from the first night we were in the park. I've been working my way backward and only got around to watching it tonight. See the date and time stamp? It's about three a.m."

Emmett tapped the forward arrow on his keyboard and the video began to play. Cruz saw a boot. A person! Someone had tripped Nettie's camera. At three in the morning? Whoever it was was kneeling practically on top of the cam. Cruz saw jeans, the hem of a jacket, and elbows. Everything else was out of frame. "Is it one of our professors?" Cruz turned to Emmett. "Dr. Downing?"

"Keep watching."

A few minutes passed. Cruz figured the person must either be eating or fixing some equipment. He saw an arm. The corner of a backpack came into view. Finally, the person got to their feet. As he stepped back from the camera, Cruz saw a knit cap.

It was a man—a man Cruz recognized.

Tripp Scarlatos!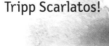

24

►**PRESCOTT FLIPPED** onto his side. Plumped his pillow. Shut his eyes. Tried to think peaceful thoughts to help him fall asleep. He couldn't think of any. Not. One.

Prescott had eaten and slept little since returning from Xi'an. And now this.

Zebra was dead.

The official word from Swan was that it was some type of lab accident involving an experiment gone wrong. Prescott knew better. What he didn't know was, did Emmett have anything to do with it? Zebra was pretty ruthless. The thought of Emmett having to . . .

He pulled the blanket up under his chin.

It may have been the path he'd chosen, but it was not one he would wish on anyone, especially someone so young. Death changes a person. Seeing it is one thing. Being part of it is something else.

Prescott spun to his other side. Plumped his pillow again. Didn't bother shutting his eyes.

"How's Jaguar?" Prescott had asked Swan when she'd called with the news.

"Fine. Shaken. But fine. We do have one glitch. The cam on Emmett's emoto-glasses is malfunctioning. We get a faint video transmission, but it lasts for only a minute or two. And there's no audio at all. It's almost like someone is jamming the signal," she said. "It could be a satellite issue, too. We're checking into it."

Prescott wasn't surprised. He knew an unwilling agent when he saw one. It could be a problem if his boss found out. Who was he kidding? Hezekiah Brume already knew that Emmett Lu was a problem.

"You're to link up with Wallaby to intercept the explorers, if necessary," said Swan. "Lion will handle Jaguar personally."

"Understood."

"And, Cobra? Lion left a message for you. Said to make sure I delivered it myself." Rough edges scraped her usually smooth voice. "He says you are not to contact Emmett Lu again."

"Understood."

Prescott flipped onto his back. He stared up at the spiral glass chandelier directly above his bed. Catching the light from the lamppost outside, dozens of teardrop-shaped crystals painted sad tiny rainbows on the wall. He shut his eyes. Tried to think better thoughts. It didn't work.

He couldn't think of—

There was one.

Piper. Silly, wiggly, blue-eyed Piper. His little girl had been gone a long time now. What was it—six years? He'd tried to fill the space between then and now because that's what he'd been told to do. They said it would get easier. It hadn't. The void had only grown. Gotten deeper. And wider. As if she were sailing one direction and he the other. Each day was a wave that took him further and further away from those chubby pink fingers and that goofy grape-juice-stained smile . . .

Prescott sat upright.

He understood now. How else does someone personally handle anything?

Of course. Hezekiah Brume was on board Orion!

25

"LET'S GET CRACKING

on the last clue before Prescott, Tripp, or anyone else from Nebula decides to show up." Sailor closed the door of Cruz and Emmett's cabin. She hung on to the wall, her flamingo slippers slowly making their way to the pair of chairs that were attached to the floor. The ship was rolling a bit more than usual. Captain Iskandar was trying to skirt the storm, but they'd caught the edge of it.

"Talk about creepy." Lani, who had settled into one of the chairs, swept her silver lock of hair behind her ear. "I still can't believe Tripp Scarlatos was following us through the Hartz Mountains wilderness for three days."

"I can," said Cruz. He was on his knees next to her, holding on to the small table. He hadn't known where or when, but it was only a matter of time before *Orion*'s former sub pilot would show up again.

When *Orion* swayed starboard, Sailor used the momentum to plop into her usual chair next to Lani and swing her flamingo feet over one arm. "What I can't believe is that he didn't try to steal the cipher."

"Who's to say he didn't?" ventured Emmett, his emoto-glasses flashing a checkerboard of pinks and yellows. "Cruz sleeps like a log. Maybe his bio force field saved the day ... or night."

Cruz was glad to see the mood frames were back. Emmett just wasn't Emmett without them.

Taking his mother's holo-journal from its sleeve, Cruz placed it on the table and held it there so it didn't slide with the ship's movement. While they waited for the journal to go through its morphing and identification sequences, Cruz swung the lanyard over his head. He carefully unhooked the seventh piece of the cipher. "This is it." He held up the pie-shaped wedge of marble. "The last clue."

His friends applauded.

They quieted down the second Petra Coronado appeared. "Hi, Cruzer."

"Hi, Mom."

"Cruz, do you have the seventh piece of the cipher?"

"I do. Here it is." Going up on his knees, he proudly held up the fragment of black marble. Cruz took a deep breath. This was his last time doing this.

His mother bent to inspect the stone.

Emmett and Sailor aimed their tablets at the holo-video, recording the clue so they could play it back. Lani, who always preferred to type it out, had her fingers poised over her keyboard. Everyone was ready for the eighth and final clue.

"I'm sorry," said Petra Coronado. "This is not a genuine piece. You have not unlocked a new clue."

"Wh-what?" choked Cruz.

The holo-video was beginning to disappear.

"Wait! Wait!" Cruz jumped to his feet, nearly falling over as *Orion* rolled to the port side. "Look again, Mom. *Please, look again.*" Cruz tried putting the piece in her hand, but of course his fingers merely passed through hers.

She was staring straight ahead, unmoving.

"Oh no!" groaned Cruz. He didn't know what he'd do if the program froze.

"Hold on," whispered Emmett calmly. "Let it catch up."

Several seconds passed, but finally Cruz's mother tipped her head downward. Her eyes locked on to the stone in his hand.

"Whew!" said Sailor. "She'll get it this time."

"It was probably a glitch," agreed Lani. "She saw it from the wrong angle or something."

It was an agonizing wait. At last, after what felt like an eternity, Cruz's mother raised her head.

Cruz held his breath, his knees feeling wobbly.

"I'm sorry," she said. "This is not a genuine piece. You have not unlocked a new clue."

"Mom?" *Orion* rolled harder to starboard, knocking Cruz off his feet. From the floor, Cruz could only stare up at the fading holo-image. "*Mom?*"

She was gone.

THE TRUTH BEHIND THE FICTION

The daring recruits at Explorer Academy have hiked through the ancient rainforests of Borneo to identify rare animals and have deployed high-tech SHOT-bots to help save a species. Though these missions take place in a fictional future world, real explorers from around the globe are jumping into action to help protect the environment. And they're each doing it in their own way—from developing new robotic technology that can operate underwater, to preserving archaeological sites for the enjoyment of future generations. Check out these six National Geographic explorers working to make lasting change.

GRACE YOUNG

Just like Cruz Coronado, Grace Young loves to explore the ocean and all that's in it. In 2014, she lived and worked underwater for 15 days as a scientist and engineer in the Aquarius underwater marine laboratory. Young specializes in developing technologies that help us better understand, explore, and manage the ocean. She's designed and built underwater robots and cameras that can record fish populations, map coral reefs in 3D, and record undersea life in slow motion. She's also helped design, build, and test-drive submersibles like Explorer Academy's *Ridley*! Even when Young can't travel to a place herself, her robots take on the job. They've been deployed in the Arctic, Antarctic, Atlantic, and Pacific to keep track of endangered species and map ice shelves to measure for climate change. She hopes that her work will help people realize that the ocean is an irreplaceable resource that we must understand and live with in harmony.

ANDREW WHITWORTH

Like the Explorer Academy recruits during their critical thylacine mission, wildlife conservationist Andrew Whitworth regularly uses camera traps for his work in Costa Rica's incredible Osa Peninsula. The Osa Peninsula is home to an astounding 140 mammal species and 463 bird species. Many of these animals, including spider monkeys, silky pygmy anteaters, and kinkajous, live and move around in the tip-top of the rainforest canopy. These species can be tricky to spot, especially at night. That's where camera traps come in: When an animal moves nearby, it triggers the camera's sensor. Strips of infrared light allow the camera to capture images at night. Tracking the movement

of these animals helps experts like Whitworth understand just how sensitive these tree-dwelling species are to deforestation. With any luck, the evidence recorded on camera traps can help save the canopy and its magnificent creatures for years to come.

ABDULLAHI ALI

Though the thylacine the recruits set out to save is extinct, we still have time to protect other species with very small wild populations. The beautiful hirola antelope is one of these critically endangered species. Native to Kenya and Somalia, only about 300 to 500 hirolas exist in the wild, with no animals in captivity. Ecologist Abdullahi Ali wants to bring the hirola back from the edge of extinction: "The first ten years of my life coincided with the hirola's greatest decline; when I heard about their plight, I had to answer the call." Ali grew up in the same area where hirolas live. He founded the Hirola Conservation Program, which focuses on partnering with local communities to restore habitat for hirola and save this unique species. A single component of this restoration work involves planned grazing, which helps to limit the spread of disease between livestock and hirolas.

ABBY MEYER

To protect our planet's incredible biodiversity, we need to ensure the preservation of plants as well as animals. Conservationist Abby Meyer is focused on the recovery of the *Brighamia insignis,* also known as *Alula* in Hawaiian or cabbage-on-a-stick. This bellflower relative once grew on two Hawaiian islands, but feral goats, hurricanes, and extinction of its only pollinator have led to cabbage-on-a-stick going extinct in the wild. Luckily, other individuals of this species are housed in botanical gardens in Hawaii and around the world. Scientists at botanical gardens are planning cross-breeding programs to preserve the health of the species. Meyer and her team plan to reintroduce new plants to the soil of their Hawaiian homeland and rebuild a wild population. Unfortunately, there are still thousands of endangered plant species. But, by learning what each plant species needs to thrive, and understanding the important role plants play in an ecosystem, there's still time to make a difference.

EDUARDO NEVES

The Terra-Cotta Army statues Cruz encounters in China show us what Emperor Shi Huang Di thought about afterlife. But what can the land itself tell archaeologists about people? When Brazilian archaeologist Eduardo Neves first started studying the Amazon River Basin, people mistakenly believed that because the area had poor soil, people couldn't farm there and create lasting human settlements. But Neves focused on Amazonian "black earth," soil that was created by indigenous people to use for farming. It preserved abundant artifacts and evidence of domesticated plants like guava, Brazil nuts, squashes, and beans. More recently, Neves has found more proof of people changing landscapes, like dome-shaped mounds of earth and stone structures. From his findings, Neves helped reframe the idea that the Amazon was only an area of beautiful plant and animal life—it's also a place with a rich human history that goes back thousands of years.

LLENEL DE CASTRO

With giant limestone towers, fossils older than dinosaurs, millions of shells, and tiger bones outside, Ille, a cave in Dewil Valley in the Philippines, is a pretty magical place. And at 250 million years old, Ille houses thousands of years of archaeology and human history within. Archaeologist and educator Llenel De Castro's projects focus on creating ways to make the history and archaeology of Ille more accessible to local people, especially children. She puts this plan into action through a museum with exhibits containing artifacts from Ille and public outreach activities with local schools. De Castro hopes to show kids just how special their own neighborhood is and to encourage them to help take care of Ille and the surrounding area. As she says, "The exploring we do doesn't necessarily mean going really, really far away; it actually means starting from where we are and the stories of who we are."

EXPLORER ACADEMY

BOOK 7:
THE FORBIDDEN ISLAND

21.8921° N | **160.1575° W**

Prescott picked up the cipher with his free hand. He stared at it in his palm, flipping the conjoined marble over with his thumb before closing his fist around it.

Cruz felt a spasm rip through his stomach. He had to do *something.* "You got what you came for," he said. "The cipher and me. Let everyone else go."

"You're forgetting the other player in our game." Prescott turned to Emmett.

Cruz felt his blood begin to simmer. "He has nothing to do with this."

"Other than being a spy, you mean—"

"He's not," clipped Cruz. "Emmett's not Jaguar. He only pretended to be so we could try to learn information about Nebula."

Prescott moved toward Emmett like a lion stalking prey. "You told me *you* were Jaguar."

"N-no." Dark gray streams of worry gushed through Emmett's emoto-glasses. "You assumed I was and I just never . . . corrected you."

Prescott twisted his neck. It cracked. "How do I know you're telling the truth now?"

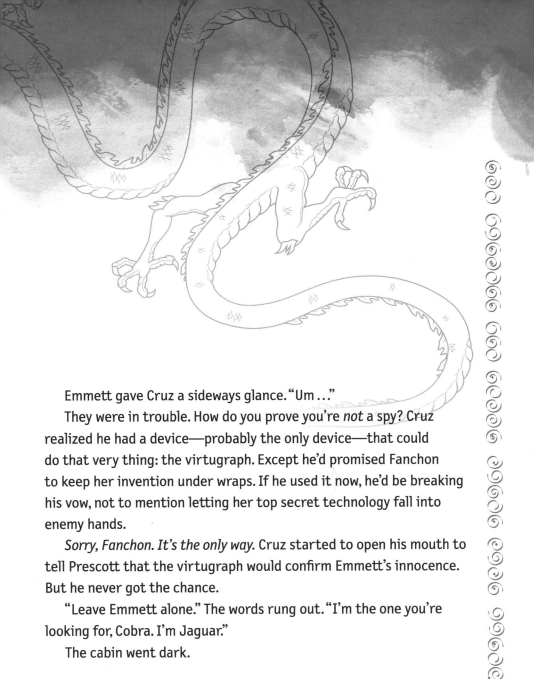

Emmett gave Cruz a sideways glance. "Um ..."

They were in trouble. How do you prove you're *not* a spy? Cruz realized he had a device—probably the only device—that could do that very thing: the virtugraph. Except he'd promised Fanchon to keep her invention under wraps. If he used it now, he'd be breaking his vow, not to mention letting her top secret technology fall into enemy hands.

Sorry, Fanchon. It's the only way. Cruz started to open his mouth to tell Prescott that the virtugraph would confirm Emmett's innocence. But he never got the chance.

"Leave Emmett alone." The words rung out. "I'm the one you're looking for, Cobra. I'm Jaguar."

The cabin went dark.

Read a longer excerpt from *The Forbidden Island* at exploreracademy.com.

ACKNOWLEDGMENTS

Writing is never a solo effort. A writer may light a spark, but you can't build a fire without help from others. I am blessed to have so many remarkable people in my life who not only fan the flames, but who also warm my heart. I wouldn't be where I am today without the guidance, passion, and wit of my delightful agent, Rosemary Stimola. She is, simply, the best. I would also be lost without my stellar editing team of Becky Baines, who can keep me laughing through the storm (while she is simultaneously calming it), and Jennifer Rees, who makes me a better writer and does it with a grace, joy, and kindness that few possess. Thank you to my National Geographic family: Jennifer Emmett, Eva Absher-Schantz, Scott Plumbe, Lisa Bosley, Gareth Moore, Ruth Chamblee, Caitlin Holbrook, Ann Day, Holly Saunders, Kelly Forsythe, Bill O'Donnell, Laurie Hembree, Emily Everhart, and Marfé Delano. A special thanks to Karen Wadsworth and Tracey Mason Daniels of Media Masters, who so brilliantly organize my book tours and can make the craziest day fun (even one that includes a car breakdown in the middle of school visits!). Thanks to all the National Geographic explorers who took the time to chat with me about their work. I am deeply grateful to those who also ventured out with me to meet young readers: Zoltan Takacs, Nizar Ibrahim, Gemina Garland-Lewis, and Erika Bergman. Each of you live your convictions and challenge me, and all you meet, to be our best selves. I am indebted to all the booksellers, schools, and libraries across the country that invited me to share the world of Explorer Academy with readers—too many to mention here, but you have my heartfelt appreciation for all that you do to inspire kids to read and write. Thank you to every young reader who has ever written to me. I keep all of your letters (so if you haven't yet written to me—do!). Thanks to my parents and family for their faithful support, especially Austin, Trina, Bailey, Carter, and my goddaughter, Marie. I love you beyond words. Finally, thanks to the most selfless person I have ever known, my husband, Bill, who tells me I can do anything and truly believes it.

Cover illustration by Antonio Javier Caparo. Interior illustrations by Scott Plumbe unless otherwise noted below. All maps by National Geographic Maps.

AL=Alamy Stock Photo; NPL=Nature Picture Library; SS=Shutterstock.
7, Nick Garbutt/NPL; 10, Thomas Marent/Minden Pictures; 14, Mark Taylor/NPL; 32, John Sullivan/AL; 33, Agami Photo Agency/SS; 63, Science Photo Library/AL; 101, Imaginechina Limited/AL; 105, Xinhua/AL; 117, O. Louis Mazzatenta/National Geographic Image Collection; 144, Ian Woolcock/SS; 146, David Gallan/NPL; 159, Mike Greenslade/Australia/AL; 208, Allegra Boverman/AL; 209 (UP), P:M Creative Lab; 209 (CTR), Andrew Whitworth/NGS; 209 (LO), Thinking Deep/Grace Young; 210 (UP), Hirola Conservation Programme; 210 (LO), agefotostock/AL; 211 (UP), Seana Walsh; 211 (LO LE), Botanic Gardens Conservation International; 211 (LO RT), Jeffrey Boutain; 212 (UP), Rafael Veríssimo; 212 (LO), Pisco del Gaiso; 213 (UP), Donna Libudan; 213 (LO), Kelvin Meneses; various (red watercolor), happykanppy/SS; various (curved tech blue design), Digital_Art/SS; various (viewfinder graphics), Stanislav Boxer/SS